The Irish Signorina

By the same author

JULIA O'FAOLAIN

The Irish Signorina

Divertimento

ADLER&ADLER

Published in the United States in 1986 by
Adler & Adler, Publishers, Inc.
4550 Montgomery Avenue
Bethesda, Maryland 20814

Library of Congress Cataloging-in-Publication Data

O'Faolain, Julia.
The Irish signorina.

I. Title.
PR6065.F317   1986   823'.914   85-28606
ISBN 0-917561-12-0

Printed in the United States of America
First U.S. Edition

The Irish Signorina

CHAPTER ONE

The car turned in through iron gates and there was the villa.

'*Bella?*' The chauffeur parked before the pale, apricot façade.

Anne agreed. '*Bella, si!*'

The stucco was luminous. Her vision blurred, then steadied and some tossed sequins became a fountain familiar from a snapshot in which her mother was sitting on its rim. There too the sun had been dazzling and the bronze dolphin spouting the water jet seemed ready to melt in its blaze. Mummy, Anne thought, looked happier in that snap than in all the years they had known each other. She had been nineteen. Today the dolphin looked less agile. Its outline had thickened under layers of water weed.

'Signorina.'

A man in livery was picking up Anne's luggage. The air was honey-coloured. Holes seemed to be pierced in it by the movement of microscopic gnats.

He waved her through a loggia, a hall and into a room so dark that she hesitated to follow and stood peering.

'La Signorina Ryan,' she heard him announce. Ree-ann was how he said it. 'La Signorina Anne Ree-ann.'

She caught smells of fruit and of warm, shut-in flesh. Then a voice answered in Italian, telling him to open the shutters. Light knifed in through the gloom revealing about twenty people sitting upright on chairs and sofas. All were old, wore black and stared unnervingly at Anne.

She smiled, but no one smiled back. One or two blinked – blinded by the inrush of light – and part of her panicked to think it could be she who was somehow appalling them. She tried to guess which was the marchesa but nobody here resembled her pictures in Mummy's old album. Well, twenty-four years was a long time – and, besides, the black of their clothes extinguished all difference in the bundles confronting her. Slowly, one of these stirred, attempted to heave its bulk from a sofa, then abandoned the effort with an acquiescent wheeze.

'Anne!' cried the bundle in confident English. 'How like your mother you look! Come in. Come over. I'm Niccolosa – the Marchesa Cavalcanti.'

Anne crossed the room while the man servant adjusted the shutters so that the light was filtered through slats. Beneath some surface scratchiness, the marchesa's embrace was like an encounter with a duvet. She clutched Anne's wrist and scrutinized her face. Her own was cone-shaped, thrusting, shrewd. She was perhaps seventy or seventy-five.

'Your mother!' she marvelled. 'Yes.' But went on staring.

Tangible as dust motes, memory eddied through the room. The gathering, it was explained, was a memorial for the marchesa's daughter, Flavia, whom Anne's mother had chaperoned when both girls were the age Anne was now.

'Twenty-five years ago, was it?'

'Nearly, oh yes, nearly!'

Heads nodded, and Anne, working round the circle, shook hands with relatives of the dead Flavia whom she had never met. Several detained her and murmured. They could have been praying. The marchesa had clearly failed to foresee the effect of bringing a girl in a pink dress into this black-garbed company. Anne could have been Flavia risen and grown young. The ladies clicked their tongues at the notion. Wasn't she, though, someone wondered, more like Flavia's friend?

E già! The little Irish girl! But this was her daughter! The Irish girl's? Well! And how, Anne was asked, was her mother? Dead too? Ai! The ceremony expanded to embrace the news.

Flavia's death, it became clear, was not recent. No. She had slipped down a crevasse on a skiing holiday some years back and now, by chance, the snows had shifted and her remains been recovered and brought home. Hands raised to touch Anne's cheek made her feel like a stand-in corpse – indeed like two corpses since Mummy now was being mourned as well. How had *she* died, someone asked. Illness? Cancer? Ts.

The marchesa put a stop to this. 'Enough!' she told her guests. 'This poor girl will think she's crossed the Styx. I didn't intend receiving you like this,' she told Anne. 'You're early. I'd supposed . . .'

At the hint, the dark chorus rose and began to disperse. Not all were women. There was a monsignor who invited Anne to drop by his presbytery for a glass of port.

'Just phone first. I remember your mother well. A sweet, bright girl.'

Anne was pleased for Mummy whose fondness for the villa had sometimes struck her as snobbish. Remorsefully, she wondered whether the snobbishness had not been hers. It had seemed degrading that her mother should remember her time here as the time of her life and keep posting greetings cards to people who might consider her a sort of servant.

'But we were on an equal footing,' Mummy had protested. 'That's what *au pair* means. Besides, I liked them.'

For a long time Anne too had liked the sound of them. Their ride-a-cock-horse name had enchanted her childhood: Cavalcanti. Her picture of them was a discontinuous jigsaw. Some bits bathed in a radiant light. Others had got mislaid.

Dislike of patronage had made her hesitate to accept the invitation which came with the marchesa's rather late letter of condolence. Then, after some months, a more pressing note arrived pleading that the Marchesa Niccolosa was ill and would appreciate a visit. To Anne, who had just sat for her BA (History), and was exhausted by half a year's cramming and mourning, a stay in Tuscany now looked attractive. She obeyed this second summons, and here she was, feeling oddly shaky and emotional.

A man of forty-five or so – in this line-up he was a youth – introduced himself as Flavia's brother, Guido, someone who – this hit Anne unpleasantly – knew private things about her mother. Guido had witnessed Mummy's adultery.

The reliable Catholic girl, brought here to keep frivolous Flavia in line, had herself slipped from the straight and narrow. Worse: she had passed the memory on to Anne as if it were a pet or a plant too precious to be let die. The thing had taken place two years after Anne's parents' marriage. By stealth. The lover, a friend of Guido's who happened to be riding in the Dublin Horse Show, had mounted Mummy in his spare time.

Don't think that way, Anne! She's dead, you know! I know.

Guido was saying he hoped Anne would enjoy her stay and that the place would not seem dull. He would have dined here on her first evening, but had, alas, to drive a flock of aunts back to Florence. He crinkled his eyes at her.

But her mind was on her mother's lover. Cosimo had been a centaur – no, a sort of god. The thought roused resentment. Anne's own dealings with men had suffered from the shadow of this legend. Passion, in Mummy's book, excused all, but without a high, hot blaze of it sex was tawdry.

'What's the matter?' one young man had demanded to know when Anne had pushed him off her. 'Am I totally repulsive to you?' he'd asked bitterly.

Not totally, no, but on a scale of ten he must rate top marks if she was to feel warrantably carried away – and desire assessed was often desire deflated. Even a strong urge, even one which had begun to soar like a fever patient's temperature could, she had found, sink under scrutiny to seven, six or even five and a half. In self-defence she must find out more about Cosimo. Perhaps meet him? She imagined a mature man with a paunch and was reminded of being taken on the knee of a department-store Santa Claus when she was really too old for this. The old man had smelled of tobacco and cough drops. He was neither strange nor magical – yet magical expectations hung about him and she had yearned to be argued out of her mistrust. Illusion is more fun than the discovery that you are sitting on the knee of someone paid to wear a red dressing gown and a cotton beard. On the other hand, it is exhilarating to find things out and Anne had in the end held it against her mother that she buoyed up a damaged myth. Mummy's reluctance to acknowledge disappointing truths had left Anne leery of fantasy – especially Mummy's. Clearly, if *she* was to justify committing adultery while her young husband was with the UN forces in Africa, Cosimo had *had* to be a god. Equally clearly, Anne's own interests were different. Chained to the rock of her mother's romantic principles, was it not her best hope that the rock turn out to be cardboard?

'Au revoir, *cara*.'

The marchesa was kissing her friends goodbye and they, their mourning tributes paid, were expanding with delicate relief. Pitching like coracles, they nuzzled around her, aged hips canting now to starboard, now to port..

'*A presto!*'

'*Ciao, bella*.'

When they had gone, she let herself collapse in a chair. She had the grey pallor of the dark-skinned and looked drained.

'Next time *they* come,' she told Anne, 'it will be for my

funeral. Oh, don't think that bothers me.' She made a soothing gesture. 'I think of myself as a traveller at an airport awaiting an unscheduled flight. That needn't mean you'll have a gloomy stay. We'll liven up my wait. Perhaps now, though, you'd better ask Bruni to take you to your room. Forgive me if I'm abrupt. One never knows how much time one has in airports.'

As Anne turned to leave, the old lady's eyelids, which looked like walnut shells, had fastened over her eyes.

Bruni was the man in livery. He threw open the shutters in Anne's room. *'Bella?'* he said of the view.

The word could have taken one a long way at the villa and indeed the view was beautiful. It was a stretch of olive groves descending a mild slope, then gathering in pale gauzy hills topped with some dark foliage which might be ilex. The air was stained green as it sometimes is in Tuscan paintings and the room was high-ceilinged with a red-tiled floor and a stove with a flue as thick, tall and slightly out of true as the trunk of a young tree.

'Is the marchesa very ill?' Anne asked.

'Ill!' Bruni agreed. 'Old. Angry. She has a lot to put up with.'

'I hope I won't be a strain.'

'Oh, you'll be good for her. It's the people who didn't come who bothered her today. Her grandson didn't and his mother – that's the marchese's wife – stayed away as well.' Bruni closed an eye. 'It's bad to gossip, but what I say is no secret. Family business is troublesome business, eh, Signorina?'

'I wouldn't know,' Anne told him. 'I haven't got a family.'

Leaning out, she saw swallows circling below. There was a word she remembered. Her reading knowledge of Italian was quite good.

'*Rondini!*' she said proudly to Bruni, who leaned beside her to look.

'*Macchè rondini!*' he contradicted. '*Son pipistrelle.*' Not swallows, bats. It was a pinprick to romancing. She laughed and so did Bruni, showing teeth the colour of chopped hazelnuts. 'It's good to have someone young in the house,' he told her. 'We say laughter nourishes. It makes you fat.'

'Why doesn't the grandson visit?'

Bruni lowered his voice. 'Politics.'

'Politics?'

'Sh!' Bruni put a hand to his lips and tilted his head sideways. There was someone at the door.

A tall, gaunt woman wearing a pod of white apron stood in its opening holding a stack of towels. She was perhaps fifty and her eroded face had scarcely a scrap of flesh on it. When she smiled, however, her teeth were as healthy as a young animal's and the flash of them picked up the light in her eyes and showed that she had once been a beauty.

'I'm Ida,' she said. 'Would you like me to help you unpack?'

'*Bene, bene!*' Bruni made a sideways move which could be construed as a semi bow. 'I'll yield the honours to la Ida.' There was a touch of mockery to this which might or might not have been malicious. He left. Ida put the towels on the bed.

'If you need anything ironed,' she offered. 'I can do it right away. You'll want to wear something dressier than what you've got on for dinner. The marchesa is expecting company.'

Anne, who had had no experience of big-house visiting, wondered how much she would be expected to tip Bruni and Ida and maybe others. What was her status here? Guests tipped, but wasn't she partly on Bruni and Ida's level? Not if Ida was going to do her ironing. She must ask the marchesa. It felt odd to have someone dancing attendance on her – but

13

then mightn't offering to do her own ironing be taken as a snub?

Ida picked a silk shirt from Anne's open suitcase. 'I'll run the iron over this. It's just the thing for this evening. Why don't you lie down? I'll hang your dresses up meanwhile so they can shake out.'

Anne lay down. This mild bullying was balm to her. It soothed memories of those last horrible months when it was Mummy who was the child – sore, neurotic, frightened – and Anne who had to do the bullying. Scenes from that time still sawed through her nightmares. The torpid half-year since Mummy's death had healed nothing. Anne had spent it cramming for her finals, numbing herself with work and failing to renew friendships dropped during the claustrophobic phase of Mummy's illness. The two had spent this in a cocoon of nervy intimacy, dining on trays, drinking tea laced with whiskey at odd hours and seeing less people than either would have done if they had been less close. The closeness predated the illness. It had begun when Anne was fifteen and her father, a captain in the Irish army, was blown to bits by a bomb he was trying to defuse.

Ida closed the shutters and said something about mosquitoes: '*Zanzare!*'

The word buzzed in Anne's ear as she fell asleep and slid into her dream as an image of dark creatures circling her in an undulating pavane.

A banging shutter awoke her and she stumbled to the window to find that the landscape had changed. Twilight was seeping up the sky. Olive leaves flicked from silver to graphite and a chill breeze snaked around her ankles. For moments she felt the anxiety that comes from losing one's bearings during sleep. Turning back to the room, she saw the skirt belonging to the blouse Ida had taken, and thought that this too should be ironed if she was to wear the outfit at dinner.

Pleased at the pretext for seeking out the reassuring Ida, she pulled on her dressing gown and went into the corridor where she tried to guess the villa's layout from the antiphony of banging shutters which had started up. She was considering going back to see if her room had a bell when a maid carrying an oil lamp came by to check the shutters. As the lamp moved, shadows stooped and flew in the clothy gloom, deforming and dramatizing the urns, nymphs and bric-à-brac with which the corridor was stacked. Anne asked where Ida did her ironing. Not here, said the girl. The generator which provided electricity for this half of the villa had broken down. Ida would be in her own flat on the other side of the *cortile*.

'Over there.' She reopened a shutter and pointed across a wide, well-like, stone-paved space. 'Take this corridor, turn left at the corner and take the stairs down.'

Anne set off and, as it had begun to rain, circled the court-yard so as to stay in the shelter of the overhanging eaves. She passed several bricked-up doors surmounted by sculpted horses' heads and guessed that these must be the stables which in Mummy's day had still been in use. Mummy had talked of riding treks, dancing parties, picnics and visits from the sons of neighbouring villas. As well as this, the household used to spend two months every summer by the sea where social life had been even livelier. The intention had been to marry Flavia off fast for she was not too bright and thought to be at risk. Not *retarded*, Mummy had insisted. No, she was a dear and not moronic or anything – just a bit innocent. Childish. An eye had to be kept on her by someone who could mingle in the young people's activities: someone whom both Flavia and her mother could trust.

'You.' Anne had liked this story which started like a fairy tale.

'Yes,' Mummy agreed, 'me. So I had to have the proper dresses and so forth. If I looked like a chaperone, Flavia wouldn't have trusted me, you see, and neither would the young men. So it was given out that I'd come to talk English to her and learn Italian myself. The nuns recommended me. I'd been head girl in my school in Tipperary and I used to wonder whether it was knowing the song that made the marchesa choose me. She was like that: half frivolous, half severe.' At this point Mummy, aroused to a limp, rueful gaiety, might begin to sing 'Tipperary'. 'Goodbye Piccadilly! Farewell Leicester Square!' Complexities of nostalgia caught Anne off balance. The fever of the sickroom flickered fretfully through these memories. Fear. Pain-killers. Consoling little drinks and consoling plunges into Mummy's past which was not, after all, truly consoling since it had finally led nowhere. While trying to ease things for her dying mother, Anne had absorbed a horror of the unlived life. Mummy's stories about the villa didn't even end unhappily. They didn't end at all. They faded out. Yet the fact that she clung to them and that, like a drowning person's dreams, they were with her at the end gave these tatters of old hope depth and brilliance for Anne. Death had got into the inconclusive sequence of anecdotes and given it the dash which had somehow evaded Mummy.

In a fairy tale, the poor chaperone, wearing dresses run up by the marchesa's dressmaker, would have carried off one of the lusty young men. That hadn't happened. Until the Cosimo incident in Dublin there had been no flirting at all. That was part of the agreement. The marchesa didn't want to have to chaperone the chaperone. One hint of gossip about *her*, she'd explained pleasantly, and Mummy could pack her bags.

'Young men are hunters,' she'd said. 'That's their nature. *Cacciatori!* It's up to you to discourage them.'

'Didn't the boys think you strange?' Anne had wondered.

'Oh yes.' Mummy was proud of this. 'They called me "the ice maiden" and "the nun". I told them I had a boy back home.'

It had been a time anyway – pre-pill – when girls flirted with prudence. Risks were high if things went wrong.

Anne, pinned in by a rush of rain, marvelled at the quaint world her mother had glimpsed.

'In those days,' Mummy had told her, 'you could be arrested for kissing on a park bench.'

'A Fascist law, I suppose?'

'Fascism was long gone. Do you think I'm your grandmother?'

Money helped then as always. There was talk of girls going to London to have a hymen implanted and to Switzerland with an inconvenient pregnancy. Mummy revelled in the outrageousness and, when Anne praised recent changes in the law for putting an end to hypocrisy, she couldn't see it at all. 'Pish and tush!' She'd say. She had the Irish preference for breaking rather than changing laws, loved things simultaneously to be and not be and had, her daughter thought, come to see obstacles to happiness as part of the happiness. 'Our sweetest songs are those which tell of saddest thoughts,' she liked to quote, and Anne could have sworn that, for her mother, 'sweet' was a synonym of 'sad'. She adored grand opera, especially *Madam Butterfly*. Maybe she identified Cosimo with Pinkerton? Maybe only impossible men appealed to her? Anyway, no fellow Anne had brought home had measured up. 'Well, *he'll* not set the Liffey on fire!' she would comment and when Anne said that was just as well, gave her a look of pity. Knowingly or not, she'd put the dead hand of her past on Anne's present and spoiled it.

As usual, resentment made Anne guilty. Mummy was dead. The disconcerting thing was how little this had changed things. Anne still found herself arguing with a ghost who was by now an extension of herself. The impulse to identify or reject – Would I have behaved differently? Am I like her? – made memory narcissistic. It was like giving your attention to someone wearing mirror sun glasses.

The rain now began to come at an angle so that the eaves were no longer a protection. Flattened into the hollow of one of the condemned doorways, she thought she heard movements behind it. A horse? How could it be? Since she was definitely getting wet, she bunched the skirt she was carrying down the front of her dress and made a run for it to Ida's door. She knocked. There was no answer.

'Ida!'

Stepping backwards into the rain, she looked to see if there were any lights in the windows then, as a movement caught her attention, looked back in the direction from whence she had just come. In a window above the bricked-up doorway a young man stood clearly visible in the still vivid dusk. One of his arms was in a sling which had been covered by a yellow scarf. Seeing her look at him, he moved out of sight. Just then Ida's door opened and Anne ran gratefully into its shelter.

Ida dried Anne's hair with a hand drier, skilfully curling the edges over a round brush. Next she ironed the blouse and skirt and sewed up a loose seam.

'This takes me back,' she said, 'to when I used to do things like this for the Contessa Flavia. She was helpless herself. A baby.'

You're a genius,' said Anne appreciatively. 'How come Flavia was a contessa if her mother's a marchesa?'

'By marriage. That marriage broke up though and she used to come back here between ... episodes. She liked us to cosset her. She couldn't survive alone, you see. But she never let herself go. She always looked smart. You could always tell who she was.'

'Who?'

'Of good stock. She always kept up her appearance.'

'You mean that ... underneath ... ?'

'Well, your mother must have told you.' Ida tapped her temple. 'Old stock ...'

'Good stock, you said.'

'Good! Of course it's good! But families are like wine. You get the odd vintage that goes right off: goes weak as coloured water or old scent.'

Ida sighed, finished strengthening the hem of Anne's dress, knotted her thread and broke it with her teeth. 'There. That'll hold. Store-bought clothes are badly finished. What else could you expect? They pay the workers by the piece and don't pay them enough. I know because my sister-in-law was a seamstress.'

'Tell me about the marchese's son.'

'Tell you what about him?'

'Why he wasn't here today.'

Ida's head shied upwards and back. 'Who's been gossiping? Bruni?'

'No.' Anne didn't want to make trouble. 'I think it was the marchesa herself who remarked on it.'

'Old people make mistakes and get stubborn about them.' Ida's own voice was stubborn. 'The marchesa's grandson is a fine boy. You'd best be getting back. Dinner's at eight. You can have my umbrella.'

Anne thanked her. Standing by the door, she struggled to raise the umbrella while holding her ironed and mended dress on a hanger. Ida came to her aid.

'By the way, who lives there?' Anne jerked her chin at the window where she had just seen the young man with an arm in a sling.

'Where? Nobody. That wing was condemned years ago. The roof is dangerous.'

Anne pointed more precisely. 'There,' she said, 'just over that door. I saw someone there just now when I came in. A man. I heard him too.'

'You couldn't have,' Ida told her. 'You must have seen a reflection in the glass. That building is bricked up and the

floors are rotten. Maybe you heard rats?' Firmly, she propelled Anne out the door. 'You'd better hurry now,' she said.
'You'll be late for dinner.'

Anne was so careful not to be late that she reached the
drawing room before her hostess. There was a guest there
already. Count Bonaccorso – Bobo – Pitti introduced himself
as a neighbour and friend of the house who was empowered
to offer her a drink.

'Gin? Grape juice? Campari?'

He was a bony man in his seventies whose suit hung flat
from his shoulders. Vertical lines predominated in his face
and achieved an effect of fluting in the folds which flanked
his Gothic nose. He had been rearranging some framed photographs on a side table and given prominence to a signed one
from the former King of Italy, Umberto.

'Our hostess,' the count spoke in over-perfect English,
lingering on the ends of words, 'may be a trifle late. A
heavy day, I gather. Like Niobe, she has been mourning her
children. Talking of children, may I ask you a question?
Would you have known from my accent that I had an Irish
nanny?'

'No,' said Anne.

The count looked pleased. His family, he explained, had
preferred Irish nannies for religious reasons, but he worried
about the accent. 'It is charming for an *Irish* person to have
an Irish accent,' he hastened to explain, 'but an Italian with
an Irish accent would be a bit farcical, don't you think?' He
added that he liked the Irish. They were so much less middle-
class than the English.

'My nanny taught me two words of Gaelic,' said the count
and gave her what his nanny might have called 'an old-
fashioned look'. Unfortunately, the words meant 'kiss my
arse': '*pogue mahone*'. He hoped Anne wasn't annoyed?

'Blame Nanny Doyle.' He shook a steeple of penitent fingers at her, but she saw that the impropriety delighted him.

'I hope you won't mind my repeating them to *you*,' said Anne, 'but, you see, your Gaelic is much too English.' She then repeated '*pogue mahone*' correctly so many times that she saw him grow a trifle vexed. 'Did she teach you anything else?' she asked conciliatingly.

'Oh yes,' said the count. 'She taught me and my father before me to wash. People of our class were all taught to wash by nannies from the British Isles. We were washing when nobody else in Italy was,' he said grandly. 'Then in 1944, the Americans came and taught the rest of the population. That's when *they* learned: 1944.' Was there a note of regret? Anne could not be sure. 'However,' the count concluded with triumph, 'the washing styles differ. They get under the shower. *We* tend to wash piecemeal with basins and bidets. Empire style, wouldn't you guess? Devised perhaps for keeping clean in the bush and on the move?'

Anne agreed with this heroic view of things and the count, restored and perhaps eager to make up for *pogue mahone*, began to talk of the Irish as dashing hippophiles. Anne was about to use the opening to ask if the count knew Cosimo when another guest arrived. This was the marchesa's doctor, a small, tobacco-coloured man in a worn silk suit who shone all over like a much-used coin. He was bald, tanned, bespectacled, smiled a lot and had just been examining the marchesa.

'She's frail,' he warned. 'More than she thinks. We mustn't annoy her.'

'It's you who annoy her,' said the count. 'Your politics ...'

'*My* politics ...'

Talk slipped into an Italian obscure with acronyms and became hard to follow as the small doctor worked himself into a passion. Saliva flew and he kept catching gobbets of it as though they were flies, wiping them with his handkerchief and excusing himself, 'Sorry, sorry!' he interjected as he removed one from the count's lapel. Recognizable words bobbed on a tide incomprehensible to Anne. 'Scandalous!' she heard, then 'cynical' and 'crime'.

'Come, come,' the count rallied in a wise voice. 'Mustn't get worked up.'

'I *will* say it!' Indignation made the little doctor's voice crack and do odd slides. 'The citizens,' he quavered, 'are castrated and . . .'

'*Dottore!*' The count barked out the word as though training a dog and the little man snapped to, his nervous system responding as clearly his raging mind could not. There was a centrifugal fragility to him. His hair, his skin and even his old silk suit looked ready to bristle and moult. His knee vibrated. His shoe tapped. He stared at the glass in his hand then raised and drank some of its stormy contents.

'You said yourself,' the count reminded him, 'that the marchesa mustn't be upset.'

'Too many people,' the doctor's voice was again on the rise, 'are protected from being upset. Censorship . . .'

'Truffles!' roared the count in his parade-ground yell. 'A little bird told me we're to have them for dinner.'

The marchesa had arrived. 'Bobo!' she exclaimed. '*Dottore!* What a pair of materialists you are! Politics and truffles! Have you met Anne?'

The two men attended her passage to what must be a favourite chair. She wore a dress which had, in motion, something of the sail, the pennant and the flag, yet fell, when she sat, into neat, shipshape lines.

Anne, she told them, had come to keep her company. Wasn't that kind? Yet who was to amuse *her*? Young people liked to dance. Did they know of any dancing partners around here now? No? She turned from prospects of dancing to memories of it. She herself had once waltzed and tangoed like a – a what? 'Help me out, Bobo.' Tilting a softly valanced chin, the old head wobbled flirtatiously.

'Like a swan?' tried the count.

This was rejected. Swans' feet were broad, she told him. Broad and flat. Hers had been high-arched and nimble. They had skimmed and careened. Her hands, bright with jewellery, made circles in the air. Now they were like roots. Gnarled. Knotted. Reaching for the earth! The humiliations of age were upon her. Even taking a bath was a hazard. Ida had to help and tonight had been in a tiresome mood. 'Something must have upset her. She nearly let me fall!' Niccolosa's bath, gamely described as a sporting event, reduced her hearers to nervous, slightly uncomfortable hilarity. 'Oh, my dears!' she confided, 'you can't imagine the slips and slides!' But when she added that getting into one's bath was a rehearsal for getting into a coffin, the three were caught on the wrong foot. 'No need to look so glum!' she scolded. 'I said the same thing to Monsignor to see if he's lost faith in the promises he's been making all these years. He promised me my just deserts and when I saw his face go glum I saw he must have grave doubts that mine will be the deserts of the just!'

By the time Bruni came to announce dinner she had them laughing again.

Next day, though sunny, was still damp. Steam was shot through with rainbows and the villa looked like blurred images of itself in Mummy's album through which Anne had once more searched for a picture of Cosimo. Many of the snaps had been poorly taken and were pocked with flecks of light. Like time itself, these had begun mutilating the faces of Mummy's subjects while they were still smiling into her viewfinder. Anne recognized spectral, chubby images of Guido and Flavia in tennis whites and a few dark, stylish ones of the marchesa.

23

Left all morning to her own devices, she mooned through the ground floor of the villa, then found her way to a walled garden where she admired staked raspberry vines and arrangements of eggplant, peppers and baby marrows. Circling back through the orchard – peaches, apricots – she came on a terrace invitingly furnished with reclining seats, iron tables and plump, terracotta nymphs. Bruni arrived at the same moment with the day's papers. The ink, he warned, was liable to come off on her fingers.

'The marchesa wears gloves to read them.'

Anne sat down, held *La Nazione* by its margins and, rejecting the first page – words like *strage* and *terrorismo* reminded her too much of home, skimmed short notices about the wine lake, the butter mountain, Polish nepotism in the Vatican and a young man who had murdered his landlady. A study had shown Italian military academies to be the most efficient institutions in the peninsula. The postal and transport services could not hope to compete. But then, consoled a journalist, Italian civilian culture had been conceived in a spirit of irony and discontent and could not be expected to bend to military disciplines. Closing her eyes, Anne thought of last night's dinner. Irony and discontent had certainly sparked through that. At one point the count had called the doctor a crass materialist.

'A good thing he is!' the marchesa had declared. 'Why else would he try to cure an old carcass like mine? If he believed in heaven the kind thing would be to send me there with a quick overdose.'

'That,' said the count who was clearly easy to shock, 'is forbidden by the Church.'

'Well, to be sure,' said the marchesa. 'If it were not, the faithful would die like lemmings and where would the Church be then?'

This reminded her of more recent pitfalls. Last time

Monsignor had taken a holiday, a missionary fresh from the tropics had preached a sermon exhorting the parish to create their heaven here and now in the guise of an improved social system. The marchesa had written to the bishop. Such fools' bargains might suit the Third World but did not, she assured him, do here. Speaking as one who would soon be on her way there, she wished to register a protest against the Church's bartering God's Kingdom for a few doubtful improvements to this Vale of Tears. Did they want to turn heaven into an upstart republic subject to tribal strife and liable to alienate one's assets?

'I mind about all this,' she told Anne, 'because I'm counting on meeting my ancestors there. Ida's been reading me their memoirs so that I'll know who they are. It's only polite. *They* can't be expected to know about *me*.' Her smile could have been whimsical or pious.

Anne got a sense of these old friends as being indifferent to what was actually said. They plucked at old themes as if weaving a long web of allusion and memory whose design was obscure to her and in whose making she could not join. The marchesa's monologues were probably variations on earlier ones made here, evening after evening, while the old count punctuated them with hisses and whistles of disagreement or approval. There was a lazy ceremony to the way they talked, a lack of immediacy, even a droning hum reminiscent of set responses. Dublin, another backwater, polished its effects in just this way, tolerating repetition in the interests of punctilio and form. It was all both novel and familiar and the web of chat was beguiling, like the spectacle of a game whose rules it would not be hard to learn and in which she could look forward to joining before long.

The doctor, who had been drinking silently, now weighed in with a lament to the effect that idealism was a thing of the past. 'I was a partisan,' he mourned. 'I was full of belief.

I believed in honesty and purity. I believed in what our songs said.'

'Well, my dear chap,' said the count, 'at my nanny's knee I learned not to ask for the moon. Nanny Doyle,' he turned to Anne. 'Irish. She taught me some words in Gaelic . . .'

'Yes, so you said!'

'*Up in the mountains,*' sang the doctor, '*under the flowers,/ Lie the best and the bravest of their men and ours.* The best are dead. Dead or old. The decent young no longer care for politics.'

'Happily!' said the count.

'Unhappily!' said the doctor. 'Though there are shining exceptions.'

'We shan't discuss them,' said the marchesa and nodded to a footman who brought in the pudding.

It was served in an amber-coloured glass bowl. Niccolosa ladled some on to a small plate then, with a smart jab of the spoon, broke the bowl and spooned some of the fragments on to the portion of pudding. The mixture was handed to Anne.

The count looked at her eagerly. 'You're surprised, aren't you?'

'Yes.'

'Hahahaha!' Nanny Doyle would surely have disapproved of her one-time charge's rowdy laugh. 'It's caramel!' he managed to explain. 'Ha!' he snorted. 'Edible caramel.'

'Quiet, Bobo. Take no notice,' Niccolosa told Anne. 'Take no notice of either of them. Company excites them. They're country mice.'

'Once . . .' began the count.

'Oh, *once,*' said Niccolosa, 'we were all worldly, but the world, *cari miei,* is backing away from us.'

'I shan't regret it.' The doctor looked sadly at his wine glass.

'Making you think that,' said Niccolosa, 'is one of the world's kinder tricks.'

Anne went back to reading her paper. SCANDALO A ROMA exploded a headline. A cabinet minister's son had fled the country a few hours before the police came to arrest him for belonging to a terrorist group. WHO TIPPED HIM OFF? asked another headline. Two of his confederates had been killed in a police shoot-out described as 'unnecessary and irresponsible'. A third confederate had escaped. DID THEY KNOW TOO MUCH? Suspicion oozed from page to page. Had the minister saved his own son and arranged to have his co-conspirators killed in order to silence testimony about this? Or about worse? Had the boy had access to government secrets? To NATO secrets? Was the CIA involved? Speculation was dizzy. There were photographs of the suspect, the missing and the dead. VATICAN CONNECTIONS? MAFIA CONNECTIONS? Might the masons be involved? By now, as Bruni had warned it might, ink had smeared not only Anne's fingers but her skirt. With the mild curiosity of the safe, she glanced at the faces of the young men who had got themselves on to police files and thought that they looked disappointingly ordinary. The fugitive terrorist was thought to have been wounded in the shoot-out and was probably lying low in some terrorist haven.

It was almost lunchtime so she bundled up the papers and went to wash her hands.

Passing the library, she heard Ida read aloud in bored tones. 'In the name of God, his mother and all the saints of Paradise,' read Ida, 'I shall now relate ...' She was beginning the memoirs of yet another of the marchesa's ancestors. Earlier this morning Anne had offered to take a turn reading, but her accent had not proven sufficiently good. Having heard half an hour of a fourteenth-century cloth merchant's diary, she was just as glad. It was less a diary really than a ledger: so many wives, dowries, surviving children, miscarriages, losses, deaths. All were reducible to figures and totted up 'for the benefit of those who shall come after me'. If the marchesa spent time with the writer of this, she was going to have a dull time in heaven.

'Reading about one's forbears can be chastening,' she had remarked to Anne. 'This man, as Ida will tell you, is glamour itself compared to some we read about on my mother's side. Very small folk. One was a fellow who made his living dredging sand from the Arno in the thirteenth century, and *his* grandson was a pursemaker whose shop on the Ponte Vecchio was destroyed by floods. Very ordinary. But tough. Ours is tough stock. Rotten branches may fall, bastard lines take over, but the stock survives. We're like olive trees. Did you know that olive trees can live up to two thousand years? Well, they can.'

The Villa Ombrosa
Wednesday

Dear Madge,

I'll be eternally grateful to you for feeding poor Puffin. He's all the household I have and I feel a rat for leaving him. What can I bring you from here? Silk? Leather? White truffles? They're better than black and a local speciality.

News? Well, I've been here nearly a week but I've none really. This place is quiet as the grave. The old lady, whom I like a lot, is out of touch with the under-seventies generation. Maybe there isn't one? Like ourselves, the Tuscans have had a Flight from the Land. That means few young people about, lots of abandoned holdings, unpicked olives and a plague of vipers. The marchesa has been instructing me about agriculture and has had the *fattore* – the man who runs her property – take me round it *three* times. Could she be thinking of offering me a job? God knows, given the job-market for BAs, I'd consider it. Scratch Puffin's chin for me and let me know what I'm to bring you.

Thanks again and love, Anne

PS. A ripple in our backwater, so I kept this back to report. We had a visit from the old lady's son, Guido, and all played charades in English. 'All' means them, me and a neighbour called Count Bobo. It seems that in their heyday, which must have been my mother's day, they were mad about parlour games: Consequences, Twenty Questions, even Murder, though the marchesa soon banned that. It's played in the dark and she saw it as an occasion of sin. She jokes about this now but one can tell she was deadly serious at the time.

Anne and two quick-eyed, fidgeting children belonging to the *fattore* had been roped in to play Monopoly with the marchesa. The game was based on Florence, and the ceramic board had been designed by Flavia at a time when she had found an alibi in pottery for some lagging on the marriage market.

'That was just after your mother left,' said Niccolosa. 'An idle girl, as the proverbs say, is at risk, so when Flavia was suddenly without a chaperone we had to invent interests for her.'

Anne hadn't known that Mummy had left suddenly. Something about the way this was said made her hesitate to ask the question the old lady was expecting. When it didn't come, Niccolosa created further openings for it, needled, waited and cast sidelong glances at Anne. She seemed to be angling – but for what? Deviousness – Anne had seen this in Mummy – might well be second nature to the dying. Truth frightens them but must be coped with, so they develop strategies for enticing it, plan measures to be taken then, with deft speed, dodge direct acknowledgement. But what was Niccolosa dodging now? Perhaps the marchesa – sometimes Anne thought of her by her title, sometimes by her first name as though they were toing and froing between intimacy and hauteur – perhaps the sick woman was simply incapable of facing anything at all head on? Any dodging could be practice for the final skirmish.

Anne had the impression – it was clear that the children did too – that Niccolosa had cheated just now at the Monopoly game. They were playing out of doors and the sun caused the old lady to lower the hoods of her eyelids so that the eyes beneath gleamed with the sliced brightness of deep wells.

'You're not playing sensibly,' Niccolosa scolded one of the children. 'You must keep some cash. If you don't, how will you pay me rent if you land on one of my streets?' Her great, spherical bust swung to and fro with the ease of one of those toys which cannot tilt over because they're weighted at the base. 'You'd have to mortgage your houses,' she warned the child. 'You'd have to give them back to Miss Ryan at a loss.'

Anne was bank because Niccolosa's stiff, old fingers had trouble sorting the flimsy, imitation banknotes.

'In their day,' Niccolosa told the children, 'the English were great bankers. So, of course, were the Florentines. An English king cheated them very badly though. Kind Edward III never paid his debts to the Bardi and Peruzzi who were both connections of my own family. Eight hundred thousand florins he welshed on: a tremendous sum! Not,' she added as an afterthought, 'that Miss Ryan is exactly English.'

The children stared at Anne and were perhaps wondering whether this made her less than exactly honest and in debt to the marchesa.

'Ha! I've landed on the via dei Bardi and shall buy it if you please, Anne.' Niccolosa collected the deeds as though performing an act of piety and conquest. It was, Anne saw, in order to land her counter on this favoured street that she had manipulated the dice. The game was a mnemonic, her purpose not to win but to be stirred.

'There!' she had tidied her assets into piles and was perceptibly taking possession not only, it struck Anne, of the Monopoly board, but of Anne herself: a vacant lot, she must feel. Emotionally vacant. Available. Was this fancy? No. Anne felt sure that what she sensed was the old lady's sly, predatory approach.

'Flavia,' said Niccolosa, as though mind-reading, 'was the wrong sort of daughter for me. It's hypocrisy to say one shouldn't speak ill of the dead. It's surely better to speak the truth about them than to forget them. We weren't suited to each other at all. Your turn.' She handed Anne the dice.

CHAPTER TWO

Anne, walking to the local village, was driven by traffic on to the edges of fields where notices forbade hunting and there might well be snakes in the grass. Wilting when she reached the tight mass of masonry which formed the village, she clung to its few scoops of shade, moving from one to the other with the gait of a chessboard knight. The village shop, behind its bead curtain, had a dense, settled smell in which she thought she recognized mosquito-repellent – she had come for this, salami and chocolate cheese. On the counter, a postcard rack spun at her touch, dissolving wedges of summer sea into marblings of foliage and red beach umbrellas packed as tight as salmon spawn.

'Dreaming of the seaside?'

It was Guido Cavalcanti.

She admitted that she had been and he regretted that he couldn't take her there. Too much work just now. He was snowed under. Maybe later in the month? She asked if he was on his way to the villa and he said, no, he was on his way *from* it: a brief visit. He had had a row with his mother. He touched Anne's elbow with one finger and guided her to the door.

'Come and have something cool to drink.' he invited. 'The local bar is modest but they will have ice.'

Sitting there, he talked of his mother's reluctance to go into hospital and of how he had upset her just now by trying to persuade her. Old people grew timorous. They got into ruts.

'Sometimes I feel I'm in one myself.'

She was prevented from saying anything to this by a disturbance on the other side of the bar. Two men were being jostled by a group of youths. Someone yelled *'Bolognesi!'* Then another voice cried: *'Bucauoli!'* The barman looked worried.

'Take it easy,' he kept repeating. 'No need to get excited!'

But the young men already were excited. 'Arse-holes, arse-holes,' went their shout. That was what the men of Bologna were. *'Buchi!'*

The two being baited tried to pretend that they heard none of this. They had ordered coffee and the barman was trying to provide it on the double. His machine sputtered as he worked its levers. Meanwhile, the jeerers kept up their chant.

'Soccer fans,' Guido whispered. 'Those two must have come in a car with Bologna licence plates. Several Bolognese have been roughed up lately in and around Florence.'

'Why?'

He shrugged. A squalid story. A surprise urine analysis had been sprung on the Florence soccer team. The results showed they were taking drugs and disqualified them from playing in an important match. The analysis had been carried out in a lab in Bologna.

'But why take it out on ordinary trippers?'

'Well what other sport is there just now in this bar? These boys,' said Guido, 'are probably unemployed.'

'You're cynical.'

'I'm not, actually.'

He walked over to the group of youths. Anne watched with some anxiety. It slid through her mind that he might wish to impress her. This was vanity so she quashed it but was still worried. An older man telling them off – if that was what he was doing – could come in for some rough treatment himself. He seemed, however, to be trying to jolly them along. After some moments a couple of bystanders joined in. Perceptibly, the tone began to change and she could see that the intention of coming to blows had dwindled – if it had ever been there.

A small convulsion in the knot of talkers gave the lie to this train of thought. A young man had a gun in his hand and, suddenly, the men around him were as still as if the scene were a photograph. The gun pointed at one of the men from Bologna who promptly spilled his coffee down the front of his suit. Anne, used to watching such things on telvision, found herself thinking that on a black and white set this would have looked like blood. Guido, she now saw, was stretching out his hand – this seemed to take minutes – to take the gun. Then he was firing it at the empty floor in the middle of the bar. It released a stream of bright green liquid. A water pistol!

Laughter exploded and someone slapped someone on the back. Guido, she noticed, looked a little silly standing there with the dripping, now obviously plastic toy in his hand. The last greenish drops looked unfortunately like pee. Like a schoolmaster caught in a practical joke! As if someone else had said this, she reacted warmly in his defence. He had been effective and quite brave, the only one in the bar to do anything useful at all. What matter how he *looked*? When he came back to her table she greeted him with praise and admiration.

'*I* was terrified!' she told him.

'No need to be,' he said, 'they just wanted someone to help them back down. Shall I give you a lift somewhere?'

The monsignor was pleased that Anne had called in. 'Coffee?' He had been wanting to chat with her, he said. 'Biscuit? *You're* surely not afraid of getting fat?'

They sipped and nibbled while the old monsignor considered his hands. Puckery and frog-like, they looked capable of slithering off on their own. The old man restrained them. There was a slight twitchiness to him today.

'Your mother,' he sighed, 'was a fine girl – woman. Of course *I* remember her as a girl. Full of spirit.'

'Yes.' Naturally he'd want to say something kind. But Mummy, in Anne's memory of her, had been a defeated woman.

'Did she suffer much – for long?'

'Some months.' She hoped he would not bring up religion: a squeamish matter.

'So death was a release?'

'Yes.'

Anne finished her coffee and wondered what he had wanted to chat about.

'More?'

'No thanks.'

He finished and put down his own cup. 'This place is a whispering gallery.' He spread his soft, spotted, priest's fingers, then gathered and respread them. 'Servants talk. They take sides.'

'Sides?'

'In family quarrels. Some members of the family may resent you. But don't worry. The Marchesa Niccolosa is independent still. *She's* in control.' He began to laugh. 'You'll have seen that for yourself.'

'I don't think I understand.'

'You don't?' She saw him check, then go on with the laugh, slightly exaggerating his easygoing manner, the way priests did. 'Ah well, I thought you might be wondering why there haven't been more visits from the family. More entertainment and so forth ... No?'

'Should I have?'

'There's no "should" to it. I just feared ...' He shrugged.

'But after all, she's ill.'

'Yes.'

'I hope it wasn't a mistake – her inviting me just now.'

'No, no. You're good for her. I'm sure of that.'

'And the family – do they think so?'

'Don't worry. I can see you have been wondering. Foreigners do. It's notorious. They find the Florentine aristocracy inhospitable – which they are. They're tight. No reason to think it's aimed at you. Listen, for the first five years that I was in this parish I was never asked out except on Fridays so that my hosts could save money by serving fish. They'd tell their other guests: "Sorry, but the Church is represented here, so we've got to mind our Ps and Qs." That way I took the blame and we all got a poor dinner. Five years of dried salt cod! *Baccalà!* The money I saved them! I was invaluable.' His laughter was easier now: a comfortable cackle. Did he feel he had been successful in throwing her off some scent? Drawn his dried salt cod across a trail? Or was he *alerting* her to a trail? It struck her that both the marchesa and the monsignor expected her to be curious about something. The monsignor had stretched his legs comfortably and was wiggling the toe of his shoe. 'Well,' he asked. 'Are you enjoying your visit?'

'Why did my mother leave here suddenly?'

'Your mother? When?'

'When she did leave – why was it sudden?'

'I suppose ... after the row with the marchesa, she would have left promptly, wouldn't she? In the nature of things.'

'I never knew there was a row. What was it about?'

'I don't feel it's up to me to tell you, my dear. If the principal parties haven't. I know the marchesa regretted ... aspects of the thing. But, well, water under the bridge, wouldn't you say? Inviting you here must be a sort of conciliation.' The monsignor's palms were extended as though showing he had nothing up his sleeve. His sleeves were black and wide enough to accommodate a ferret in their clothy cavities. Nothing, however, fell from these. 'Discretion,' he pleaded, 'has to be our first concern. As priests, I mean: why would anyone – you, for instance – trust us if we didn't have it? Listen,' he suggested, 'why don't you ask the marchesa to talk to you? It's time you and she talked.'

'About what?'

Once more the monsignor spread his empty sleeves.

'Play poker with her,' he advised. 'Bluff and you may find out.'

That evening, however, there was no chance to discuss anything with the marchesa. Her son was back. The Marchese Guido. And he was in a party mood! Come to win her round. Bruni told Anne as she came in through the loggia, but she had already guessed something was up. The voltage of life at the villa was perceptibly heightened. Dogs were frisky; doors ajar; servants raced about. Guido had brought a case of champagne and a crate of boletus mushrooms which he carried into the kitchens and began to discuss with the cook. They must be done whole on the grill. With catnip. Then served just as they were. No fuss. No sauces. They were too good for that. Prime specimens. Succulent. Firm and, to be sure, local. Produce from outside Tuscany wasn't worth eating. He sniffed his own gift with pleasure and arched his palms to the shape of thrusting mushroom caps. Meanwhile, the champagne should be cooled. What else was for dinner? He discussed the menu, then came out to chat with his mother.

Niccolosa was energized. 'What are we celebrating?' Her back straightened and she had even, Anne noticed, applied a rakishly inaccurate dab of lipstick.

'My news.'

'What news?'

'A big case!' Didn't she read the papers? 'Really, Mamma, haven't you heard of the scandal that's rocked the government? About the cabinet minister's son who skipped the country?' There was to be major litigation and Guido had been engaged to represent the father. Yes. The cabinet minister! He laughed at his own boasting. 'But if you will be such a country mouse, Mamma, how am I to impress you? I have to resort to gross self-promotion.'

His mother questioned him greedily and kept breaking off to explain things to Anne. Guido had brought life to the villa. The big world! How had he managed to get away at such a time? No, save the details for dinner. The count would be interested. So would the doctor. Unless it was all too secret for talk?

'Have those two moved in?'

'O, caro, if I relied on my own family to keep me company ...' The complaint was coquettish. She explained that she needed the doctor. He might be rough and ready but she was lucky to have him here in the village. 'And I'm lucky to have Anne.'

'Oh indeed!' Guido had the gift of focusing totally on whoever he talked to. Now it was Anne. 'I can see you've rejuvenated my old mamma! Youth is contagious, vero, Mamma?' His sigh lingered in the air. Then he said something in Latin. A bit of a poem with the word for roses in it and you could guess that the roses were wilting or dying or about to die. He was looking at Anne as he said it so that the notion of youth's brevity became attached to her who was enjoying its bloom while he, having survived it, seemed younger than young. Like a maiden in some old ballad, he had consigned her to peril.

The marchesa, on the other hand, was freed from it. She had perked up enormously and was a new woman or, more likely, had revived the woman she must once have been. She kept touching her son's knee and wrist as he sat next to her and laughing or trying to draw Anne into the chat. But Anne knew nothing about Italian politics.

Guido would not have this. He would *prove* to her that she knew as much as she needed. Really! He himself, he assured her, was not especially in the know. What did she think she didn't understand? This new scandal? Its background?

'Just read the papers. That's where illusions are created – which then become real. There's more illusion to politics than to religion. I'm serious. Do you know what has kept my party in power for the last thirty-five years? Fear. Fear of Communism. That's all. It's the head and tail of our policies. We try to keep it alive and the CP tries to lull it. That's all you need know.'

His mother clicked her tongue off her palate: thth, a Florentine sound meaning 'no'.

'Yes,' contradicted Guido.

'Thth!'

But his outrageousness amused her and he had a clown's licence.

'Remember 1948,' he challenged, 'remember, Mamma, when the priests threatened you all with hell fire if you didn't vote against the CP? Then they opened the convents and brought out the senile, the insane and the enclosed religious to swell the vote. I was a twelve-year-old altar boy and they had me helping with the wheelchair cases.'

Niccolosa's tolerance was running out. 'They needn't have done any of that,' she said sharply. 'They'd have won anyway. People really feared the Reds then.'

'Exactly! Now they don't. Now the terrorists are a gift and a boon to us because people associate them with the Communists – who naturally hate their guts, so whenever they commit an atrocity the fear-count rises and our party gains. Could it be that *we* have double agents working inside the terrorist ranks?' An artful pause. 'People, maybe, like my client's son?'

'You don't mean ...'

'I don't know. I'm not giving away secrets. Nobody knows.'

Guido had a subtle face. It would remind you of portraits by – was it Titian? Bellini? Dark-clad gentlemen whose hands fondled a rose or a sword hilt while they looked out at the viewer with wise, sad, sensual eyes. Looked out at you from the imprisoning fusc of the canvas with its heavy gilded frame.

'But you think the son could have been ...?' Niccolosa was fascinated.

'About his father's business? That will certainly be said. We'll have to cope with that. And other speculations. Not with the truth. We'll never know it and if we did it would make no difference. Whether he was a stool pigeon for us or stealing our secrets for the Red Brigades, either way, he's now a liability. The party will want him out of the way. Him *and* anyone he talked to.'

'You're shocking Anne,' said Niccolosa with robust amusement. 'She comes from a country far from the firing line. They've never had to make hard decisions.'

'Well, neither am I making them,' said Guido. 'I represent the boy's father who wants his son kept alive. We hope to persuade the party brass that the boy knew nothing.'

'You're shocking her,' said his mother, 'and she thinks you're lying.'

'I would be,' said Guido, 'if I pretended to be innocent about what goes on. To rescue someone caught in troubled waters one must study the currents.'

His mother laughed. 'One doesn't quarrel with the rules of the game of whist.' She looked at Anne. 'Do you know who said that?'

This session, like the Monopoly game and the visits to Niccolosa's farms, was turning into a pedagogical exercise:

part of the education the old lady had apparently taken it into her head to give Anne.

'No,' she admitted.

'And what do you think of it?'

'Well, if it's played for bloody stakes . . .'

'*My* stake,' said Guido, 'is a boy's life and my party claims to play for the Western Way of Life – talking of which, shall we open the champagne?'

Anne imagined this scene from the outside: the champagne, the slightly scuffed elegance of the room, the laughter. Caption: man of the world relaxes with indomitable old lady and a girl . . . She could think of no quality to attach to the girl. Who or what was she? Nothing yet. She was empty, flexible, waiting to acquire opinions and a definite character. Perhaps, after all, youth *was* a precarious time?

Guido struck her as surprisingly free of self-importance and she could barely believe he held the position his mother claimed he did in the ruling party: a grey eminence, much consulted, rarely emerging or showing his hand. Here he was all ease and fizzed with jokes which, though probably old, were new to her. Crackling like straw beneath a bonfire for burning idols, they excited like the breaking of a taboo. This fancy was his, not hers and, though they laughed over it, she was persuaded too.

'Actually,' he elaborated, and slid the champagne cork from its bottle as easily as if it had been the yolk of a hard-boiled egg sliding from its casing of white, 'actually, half the jokes in Rome go back to the days of the early Popes. Even *then* they were recognized as ways of letting off steam: safety devices.' Had she heard of Pasquino, he asked, the statue on whose torso Romans used to pin lampoons – *pasquinades* – about the current Pontiff and his court? 'We three, laughing over our champagne,' he said with sudden sobriety, 'are in a long and pessimistic tradition. Ours is sad laughter.'

He had a Harlequin face with substitute sets of wrinkles. In repose all lines were delicately visible. Ready to come into play they gave him an air of sensibility – also of being two-faced.

The notion tumbled out: 'Do you mean you're two-faced?' Anne blushed for her unretractable rudeness. 'I'm sorry,' she exclaimed, appalled.

But Guido didn't mind. 'Don't you think,' he asked gently, 'that the world is complex enough to require at least two faces of us?'

He was a good-looking man: tall and lean with hair the colour of dimmed brass, not at all like the northern notion of the typical Italian. But, as Mummy had often told Anne, Tuscans weren't.

He and his mother continued to joke and glitter and struck Anne as too feverish and maybe fragile, and she began to wonder whether the true reason for her son's visiting at such a time was that Niccolosa was even sicker than she had let Anne suppose.

However, the flare-up of excitement was brief. At dinner, later, with the doctor and the count, the Cavalcantis were discreet, even subdued and this made Anne feel privileged and close to them.

Next morning Guido was gone and the villa quieter than ever so that, in retrospect, the evening's gaiety seemed utterly alien to it. In Anne's mind, however, there lingered, like rainbow petrol puddles on a deserted road, a sense of life as encapsulable in high-coloured, stylish, faintly bitter jokes.

The Signora Marchesa would let nobody nurse her but Ida, and Ida was proud she had the strength. You needed that if you were to help the invalid upstairs or down or even to prop her upright in her bed. Lately, the old lady's bones had grown brittle and the poor, bloated flesh around them was so much jelly. You could bruise it as quick as look at it, and whoever took over on Ida's days off was likely to leave the patient looking as if they'd beaten her. They lacked Ida's technique. The trick was to thread your hands through the sick woman's soft armpits, then raise the body steadily while making sure you didn't strain yourself and drop it. Another method was to seat her on a flat cushion which could be pulled about the bed like a sled or coaster. Above all, you needed patience which was one thing life had taught Ida and it was a good thing it had, for it had certainly not taught it to the marchesa. To be sure, she'd had her share of tribulation, but, say what you liked, money was a buffer. Even during the war, when German officers had been billeted in the villa, they had kissed her hand and treated her like a lady. Ida knew this from the housekeeper who'd been here at the time. A title commanded respect and money oiled the wheels. It made Ida smile when the marchesa praised herself for having survived all she had. Oh, she had fortitude. She was a fine woman. *Una gran bella signora!* Who'd deny it? But when she talked of the hard life she'd led – well, God love her, she didn't know what 'hard' meant. Ida's sister-in-law could have told her. Not that the marchesa would have listened. She couldn't stand to hear Rosina's name.

'She is *not* your sister-in-law!' she always interrupted when Rosina's name came up. 'Your brother isn't married to her, so she's a mere concubine. I can't see why you can't get that through your head.'

To Ida's mind, Rosina was ten times more married than women who'd had priests and mayors mumble and drone over them. Rosina hadn't wanted the ceremony because a wife wasn't eligible for a pension the way a housekeeper was. She'd persuaded Ida's brother to register her as his employee and pay her stamps throughout his earning years, and, now that these were over, he was cock-a-hoop that he had, for the social security was coming in very handy. He'd had a lot of bad luck and without Rosina's foresight the two would be in a nice mess. But try explaining that to the marchesa! 'Concubine!' she said as if the word had a bad taste.

The truth was that she was afraid Ida would leave her and go to look after poor Rosina who'd had a bad operation.

'The woman's no relative of yours,' she kept insisting and wasn't above hinting that Ida should remember on which side her bread was buttered. *She* wasn't long for this world. Was it too much to expect loyalty from someone whom she had always regarded as a friend and remembered in her will?

Ida didn't hold the marchesa's selfishness against her. The poor lady suspected her household of having grown used to the notion of her death – which, to be sure, they had. With the best will in the world, they had to look to the future. Understandably, she was quick to spy out such thoughts and find them hurtful. Her selfishness, thought Ida, was part of her will to live. Healthy. Natural. At the same time, it was depressing – for what good was a will to live in the dying? Wouldn't acceptance be better than this flying of nature in nature's face? Up to now, Ida had felt that her association with the Signora Marchesa shed credit on them both. There was mutual respect. There was tolerance and a recognition of the limits beyond which neither could push the other. Their solid, Tuscan good sense uplifted and reflected well on both.

All this made the dying woman's frenzy to drag her life beyond its useful span upsetting to Ida. It looked as if her patient, blinkered by a lifetime's privilege, had less knack for facing up to things than a farm animal. Shaken, Ida took out her feelings on the plumber.

The trouble turned on a radiator he had been asked to install in the marchesa's bedroom. He was a boy from the local village who considered the job in silence for some time, then stated flatly that he never took money under false pretences and would rather say 'no'. It couldn't be done, he'd added when questioned, without spoiling some fine panelling and was 'hardly worth it now'.

'Couldn't you get along with a stove for the time you'll be here?' he'd asked the sick woman and blinked doltishly when Ida made angry signs at him from behind her back. Later, when she told him off, he had grown cheeky. 'Too good to die, is she?' he'd asked, echoing the very comment which Ida had to keep suppressing in her own head.

The marchesa, who hadn't been outside the villa gate in eighteen months, had grown increasingly indifferent to people outside it and possessive of those within. These included her son — though he only came on visits, the count, the doctor, Ida and now, surprisingly, the Irish girl. It was surprising because Ida wouldn't have expected her to have the energy to get interested in someone new. What happened was that the girl, who must never have met anyone like the marchesa, was impressed by her and this pleased the marchesa.

'She's a game old lady, isn't she?' the girl had said and that had acted as a tonic when Ida reported it back.

What struck Ida even more was the girl's helpfulness in the sickroom and the speed with which she picked up the invalid's finicky requirements down to remembering that she liked her bedroom door left ajar at an angle of forty-five degrees, her coffee tepid, her mineral water at room temperature and her pills neatly quartered before she swallowed them.

'Oh, my mother was the same,' said the girl. 'I like helping,' she protested when Ida said she mustn't. Then she added: 'I think maybe I'm making up to myself for not having been nice enough to *her*. She was maddening a lot of the time and since she died I've had depressions and nightmares. This helps.'

The arrangement suited Ida, who could now take time off with a clear conscience. If Rosina got sicker, she might take off completely. Blood was thicker than water and her brother's life companion had nobody else to help her. Let the marchesa rail. *She'd* be well looked after, whatever happened. To be sure there was the danger – Ida didn't know whether there really was, but you could never tell – of a deathbed infatuation, the girl's insinuating herself into the invalid's affections, undue pressure and a changed will. Ida had worked with the rich too long not to think of that. With more loyalty than the marchesa perhaps gave her credit for, she had taken it upon herself to warn the family. She had telephoned the Signorino Neri, though so far, that hadn't been much use. His grandmother wouldn't see him.

'That boy's turned into a Red and a robot,' was all she'd say. 'I don't care half so much about his being a class traitor – which he *is*, Ida – as about the way he freezes my mind. He used to be a charming child but I'm too old and too tired to listen to robot talk. That boy doesn't *think*. He echoes. I'm nearly dead. Why should I have to listen to dead speech?'

'He's young,' said Ida. 'He hasn't had time to think for himself yet.'

'Well, and I'm old. Why should he lecture me? Besides, if he wants to come, he must be after something. A legacy? You can tell him I've cut him out.'

'He's not after anything.'

'Then why does he want to come? He should know we only quarrel. I shan't see him.'

Ida had left it at that. The boy was a good boy. His heart was in the right place but he lacked tact with his grandmother which, as Ida had tried to point out, could cost him dear. He didn't get on with his father either and this year wasn't even at the university but running round with a lot of excitable youngsters like himself. Never mind. Ida had done her duty. She'd told him to tell his mother about the girl. It wasn't that Ida had anything against the girl; *per carità*, no, but her loyalty was to the family. If she hadn't spoken directly to the Marchese Guido it was because of something the old marchesa had let slip. Not that you could put much trust in a lot of what she said these days. She had moments of being less than quite herself.

'Eithne,' she'd said, 'Eithne . . .'

Ida hadn't paid attention at first. Then she'd remembered that that was the girl's mother's name.

'Like mother like daughter,' the marchesa went on. 'The mother was trouble. Sweet, biddable – but a handful of trouble in the end. Guido was looking at her last night in that way he has.'

'Looking at whom?'

'Eithne. Eithne. The Irish girl. She's supposed to be looking after Flavia and instead . . .'

'What?'

'I can't talk about it. Oh, how tedious one gets lying in bed.' Ida couldn't tell whether this was a complaint or an apology. 'Self-absorbed,' said the marchesa. 'I've been think-ing about the past. Our own past, my past,' she explained, 'not the memoirs. Not history, though I suppose it's all history now; all gone now. We thought too much of the future, Ida, and now where is it? Where?' The marchesa's lip trembled, but whether with laughter or sorrow Ida couldn't tell. 'What's the point of sacrificing and putting off? Tell me, Ida, do you see any?'

'There is a future,' said Ida. 'People plan for it. Farmers plant for it. You have to assume . . .'

'Ah, you think I'm selfish? That I think the world ends with myself? I was never like that. But . . .'

'But?'

'I may have interfered too much . . . Passion has rights too.

I'm not senile,' said the marchesa, reading Ida's mind. 'But some passions are irrepressible. Dam them up in one place and they'll emerge in another. Do more damage. Look at what happened to poor Flavia.' The marchesa's eyes were wet. 'I blame myself,' she said agitatedly. 'There are things you don't know about, Ida. Nobody does. I can't discuss them. But I've arrangements to make. I need advice. I need to put things right now – and how can I while new troubles start up right under my nose? I can't talk. I'm ill. I want my pudding right now. Before lunch. Tell the cook to send it up. I have a bad taste in my mouth from all those medicines. Bitter. They repeat. Everything repeats. I need something sweet.'

Ida went down to the kitchen to find that the cook had just put a sweet soufflé into the oven. No, of course it wouldn't be ready *before* lunch! Who had ever heard of such a thing! Why hadn't Ida told him sooner? A Grand Marnier soufflé gone to waste! The kitchen staff would have to eat it. *Porca mattinata!* She hadn't known? Well, all right, but he couldn't conjure puddings out of thin air. The marchesa would have to be satisfied with a sliced peach in sugared wine.

'I don't call this a pudding,' said the marchesa when Ida brought it to her. 'Oh, Ida, I'm a tedious old thing! You're not planning to leave me, are you? Remember you *promised* not to!'

Ida, who had made no such promise, saw that if she didn't deny this, the marchesa would take silence for consent and hold her to it and that if she did there would be a scene. She was pondering the alternatives when her patient started to sob.

'I'm upset,' wailed the invalid. 'I shouldn't be upset. It could kill me and I've got to stay alive to stop ...'

'What? What's the matter?'

'Guido and that girl – Eithne, Anna – they're falling in love.'

'Which girl? Are you sure? You may be mixing things up.'

'Ida, I'm not senile! I may forget names but I know when people around me are in heat. God knows I've been watching them get into the condition all my life. I'm like a dog-breeder. The trouble I had fighting off males from Flavia and then ... Like a dog-breeder! Why do they do it? Why do they *need* it? Bonaccorso Pitti has been in love with me for fifty years and have I taken a blind bit of notice? No, I have not. And are he and I any the worse for that? Are we less good friends? No, but these others ...'

'Signora Marchesa, are you sure you're not imagining ...'

'My imagination, Ida, does not run to sex. There's enough of that around without imagining more. If there's one thing the world needs less of, let me tell you from long experience, that's it. I *saw* it. It was in his eyes and in hers too. They were like partners dancing to their own music: in time, in rhythm. Up, down, feverish, frightened but keeping time. They felt it. They may not have said a word about it but it has happened. It's a fatality. *Not* saying anything is the worst sign. Still waters run deep. Silence, Ida, a slow, swollen, sulky silence is the worst sign. It's a malady and I know the symptoms – oh, do I know them! When you see two people in its grip there's little to be done. They become like clams. Hedgehogs. They turn inwards and will listen to no tune but their own.'

'Signora Marchesa, does it matter? Really?'

'Ida!'

'Seriously, forgive me but – what's the use of upsetting yourself? Getting excited ...'

'Oh, but there are things you don't know, Ida, things ... aspects. Oh, I need advice and my son is useless now. I was going to consult him – but not now. Maybe the monsignor would be the best man to turn to? Make an appointment with him, will you, Ida. Ask him to drop round. Tell him it's confidential. No, perhaps I'd better talk to him myself. Bring me the telephone.'

'You're excited,' Ida reproached. 'That's bad for you. Hadn't you better wait?'

But the marchesa wouldn't wait. As she left the room, Ida could hear her talking in little gasps and spurts into the telephone. Later, she telephoned her lawyer too and made an appointment with him. Her will, Ida supposed.

'Life lived like this,' said the marchesa to her later, 'is like watching a shadow-play. I suppose one gives oneself too much importance always? Maybe I was responsible for less than I thought?'

'One usually affects things less rather than more,' said Ida. 'Most things happen by accident.'

The marchesa laughed. 'Maybe the real fear is of not counting at all? Being cut off? Forgotten?'

'That happens to the poor,' said Ida, thinking of her brother and sister-in-law.

'It happens to the dead,' said the marchesa.

Anne borrowed Niccolosa's second car and drove to Florence where she did time in a treadmill of blazing metal, circling the city's centre in search of a parking slot. Whenever she saw one, a car seemed to lurch recklessly ahead of her, then, at the risk of a crash, with a millimetre to spare, skid into it. The drivers had the reflexes of matadors. Their cars had dents. When at last a parking attendant directed her into a space, her dress was clinging to her thighs and shoulder-blades and her spirit so bruised that she meekly handed over an exorbitant parking fee.

Shaking, she went into a bar choppy with reflections of the brilliance outside and ordered a lemon juice with ice water. As the liquid slid down her throat, she felt her whole being concentrate on it. The rest of her body felt numb and it struck her that something similar was happening to her mind. Like water mixed with lemon juice, her personality had been overwhelmed. She was filled with the flavour of Italy.

Mummy's chat had prepared this surrender.

'You'll see,' Mummy had prophesied. 'You'll hear ...' Trained like a catechumen, Anne had been all readiness, all tuned up.

Outside, heat fell on her like a blanket. There were smells of dust. Palaces of rusticated stone, built by cloth merchants and usurers and chastened feudal barons, were as stolid as ledgers and closed like clams. There were grilles on ground-floor windows, and shutters had been drawn against the heat. Florence was excluding her. It was excluding everyone and she hugged to herself her privileged insider's memory of yesterday evening.

She had a map and found that she had followed it to the Cavalcanti palazzo whose string course appeared to be crumbling and whose courtyards were austerely concealed. Inside – she had been told – were loggias fragrant with potted shrubs. The thought of this secret elegance entranced her and she was lingering in the hope that someone might open a door and give her a glimpse of it when the thought struck her that one of the villa servants who came here regularly with supplies of fresh produce might see her hanging about and wonder. Niccolosa had failed to suggest that Anne call here while in Florence.

At that moment the palazzo door did open and three middle-aged ladies came out. Any one of them could be Guido's wife. Embarrassed at being caught staring, Anne turned and stepped through the bead curtain of a small teashop. Maybe Guido himself would appear behind them and introduce and shame her. If any of them had happened to peep out, they could have seen her watching the place for the last ten minutes.

'I'll have an éclair and a coffee,' she told the waitress and sat down at a table. This, it came back to her, was a shop which Ida had recommmended highly for its pastries and sweets.

Next minute the bead curtain parted and in walked the three ladies. Anne opened her guide book and pretended to be absorbed. They seemed unaware of her and were choosing cakes. When they had made their selections, they sat at the next table.

'Pff!' said one and fanned herself vigorously. 'I feel I've earned these. What a *mood* Maria-Cristina is in! And that tisane she served! It tasted like soaked grass. She must have had it in her cupboard for a year.'

'Well, she has her troubles. There seems to be a blight on that family,' said the fattest lady who, like the other two, was wearing fashionably creased linen. The creases, however, had disappeared as she sat, smoothed away by the expanding pressure of her flesh.

Watching covertly in a mirror, Anne could see why it was expanding. In under two minutes the woman had put away a *Saint-Honoré* and a hazelnut liqueur cake. A jam tart and a meringue waited on her plate.

'Have you heard the latest about ...?' The voice sank to a susurrus so idiomatic and confidential that Anne was lost.

'*Ma ...*'

'Ththth!'

'Guido,' said one of the women clearly, 'must be worrying lest that delinquent son of his embarrass him now that he's got this prestigious case.'

'Oh *bella*, if the sins of the sons were to be visited on their fathers, his own client would be out of office.'

'*Isn't* he? Won't he be?'

'No, they say ...'

'Shsh!'

The ladies' heads nuzzled close. Their voices sank and for

a while all Anne could hear was the odd fragment of an injunction to stop tantalizing and tell.

After some minutes, having presumably moved to less highly classified gossip, they emerged from their huddle.

'Of course,' the fat one chased a few final crumbs with her pastry fork, 'the old marchesa is to blame for a lot. Niccolosa. She imposed that marriage on Guido and Maria-Cristina. It never worked. Not for a day. Neither really wanted it and they're too closely related.'

'Maybe that's what's wrong with the son!'

'They say cousins marrying is a sign of meanness. It's a way of keeping assets in the family.'

The ladies tittered and bent over their plates. Presently, they began to talk of something else and after a while Anne paid and left. She felt the exhilaration of a poacher who has not only escaped detection but bagged an unexpected bit of game: a specific and interesting fact. She could not have said why but she was jubilant to hear that Guido's marriage had not worked ever, not for a single day.

A graffito caught her eye: VIVA L'IRA. She wondered whether it meant solidarity with the Irish Republican Army or the Italian word for wrath. Whose? God's? The people's? It had a fine ring to it, but Anne had been inoculated early against such seductions.

Her father was the reason. She had a shamed suspicion that if he had lived she might have found him dull. Upset by this, she had combed her memory for something to keep her picture of him from fading to a dim silhouette equipped with a blinking grin. She remembered that he had believed greatly in honesty. Paying your debts, he had often said, was the basis of society. Usually, nobody bothered to argue.

When he died, an Irish army officer killed by a bomb he had been trying to defuse, the issue was too unclear to be memorable. The bomb had been planted by a shadow army which claimed the same origins as his own but had cornered the market in romance. Nobody spoke up for *his* comrades at Hyde Park Corner or the Place de la Bastille, but IRA supporters were photographed there regularly. On bank holiday weekends they marched through the capitals of Europe with groups like the Mojahedin, Free Turks and Chilean refugees. In Dublin, they had held debates at Anne's university and raised money, passing round collection boxes while girl students with pretty hair plucked at stringed instruments. Sometimes the girls sang love songs:

> The red rose whispers of passion,
> And the white rose breathes of love;
> O, the red rose is a falcon,
> And the white rose is a dove.

Anne had gone along once or twice intending to engage in the debate but saw that the issue of honesty would be impossible to introduce. Honesty, she would have been asked, on whose behalf? The debaters' voices had been excited and she saw that their cool arguments were camouflage. The red rose had their allegiance. Their end was everything to them and a few fathers getting blown to bits didn't worry them at all.

Italian dissident groups were likely to be much the same and she looked coldly at their graffiti too.

In the Uffizi Gallery she walked through rooms full of landscapes very like the ones she had driven through to get here. The foregrounds were posed, often passionate indoor scenes from religion or mythology but it was the backgrounds which drew her eye. Miniature paintings within paintings, these peeped through windows and arcades, reflecting everyday vistas of pale horizon, dark cypress, golden house fronts, gulleys, cliffs, olive groves and towers awash in that same spinach-water light which had heralded the storm on her first evening. Here, under a perfecting glaze, was a distillation of Tuscany so vivid that when she came out of the gallery her sense of art and actuality had fused into a radiant banderol which seemed both to enwrap and ripple through her mind.

'Well,' asked Niccolosa at dinner, 'did you enjoy the paintings?'

'Oh,' cried Anne extravagantly, 'I'm in love with those landscapes. In love with Tuscany. It's the *coup de foudre.*'

'*Colpo di fulmine* we say here.'

'*Colpo di fulmine* then.' Politely, she repeated the words.

Gaining momentum, they began to echo and unleash a tumult in her imagination. She was inflamed.

'I'm glad you feel that way.' Niccolosa looked as alert as a gun dog and might, Anne feared, sniff out Anne's obscure, still burgeoning thoughts. 'You love it,' she approved. 'So do I. One way or another, it will go on. That,' she waved a hand towards the dusky out-of-doors, 'as you saw yourself today, looks much as it did five hundred years ago, and matters more to me than the politics which so exercise my son and grandson.'

'You wish one of them would come back here to farm?'

'There is no hope of that.' Niccolosa's leathery mouth closed with a snap. 'None. Farming is my hobbyhorse. Politics is theirs. Not that they agree even about that. Neri wants to change the system, Guido to patch it up.' She sniffed dismissively. 'I've seen what people thought to be great political changes matter little in the end. Pff!' Niccolosa despised the transitory. Vineyards were tangible. 'My son and grandson disagree.'

'Is your grandson ... wild?' The word made one think of students stealing policemen's helmets, but Anne doubted if that sort of wildness existed any more.

Niccolosa was scrutinizing her attentively and had perhaps guessed that she had asked about the man who didn't interest her.

'Wild?' She considered the word. 'He got into trouble at the university. Some nonsense about a strike, but in my opinion he's more dull than wild. If you were to tell Neri the story of the Sleeping Beauty, he'd ask about the Prince's income and who elected him.'

CHAPTER THREE

Bruni complained of the *afa* and Anne, looking up the word, found 'sultriness, breathlessness, oppressive heat'. The shuttered villa preserved each morning's freshness until the following night, but the air outside was hot and the glare cut like a scythe. 'Tedium' was another suggested meaning for *afa*. So were 'nausea' and 'disgust'. On the terrace, she came on a dead lizard and a procession of scavenging ants. Decay moved fast here, shrivelling dead matter as if in an oven – and, indeed, the noon landscape had the hard-edged outlines of a kitchen.

After lunch, everyone withdrew for a siesta and Anne went to the library for a book. Since nobody was likely to see her, she had taken off her shoes and walked barefoot along the corridors, enjoying the contact of age-smoothed tiles against her naked soles. The library, like the rest of the villa, was shuttered but she knew where the nearest lamp stood in relation to the door and had her hand on its switch when she noticed a small spot of light skittering along a shelf of books. For a moment she supposed it to be coming from a loose shutter, then saw that it was too mobile for that. Abruptly, it disappeared and there was a sound of something falling. Her finger pressed the switch and the room lit up.

Just yards from her a young man stood holding a book. A small flashlight was rolling by his feet.

They stared, perhaps in equal shock; Anne heard herself

give a cry, then saw that this was not a burglar. He had recovered too quickly and was already too much at ease. Besides, she had begun to guess who he must be. Who he was *not*, it struck her at the same moment, was the young man she had glimpsed in the window over the old stables.

'You're Anne.' He held a hand out to be shaken, approaching at such a gravely soothing gait that it was clear she herself must be the very image of alarm. 'Ida's told me about you. I'm Neri, the grandson of the house. Hullo.'

Since he had said this with the nannified English diction used by the Cavalcantis and their friends, she guessed it must be true.

'Hullo.'

The flutter of the extinguished flashlight was reproduced in his smile, his eyes and in a kind of quick wiggle of head, hips, hands which was obviously a trick of his: a total body gesture as if he had mobilized his whole self in a laugh. He had that apparently boneless grace of very young animals and she remembered Bruni saying that he was just twenty. His hair was a brighter version of his father's. Blond and bubbly, it suggested antennae and heightened the appearance of volatility which seemed to be the very essence of him. There was a millimetre gap between his front teeth. With a lunge, he scooped up the torch.

'I'm the light-bearer.'

'Lucifer?'

'Well, banished like him, but not so wicked. Or perhaps for my grandmother I am? His sin was pride, wasn't it? I suppose failing to get along with *her* must seem the ultimate in wickedness.'

'I'd say sneaking in here behind her back was worse.'

'Mm. Are *you* going to play the angel with the flaming sword? I hope not.'

'You mean give the alarm? I don't know.'

'A dilemma? I might be a drug addict. Nowadays one never knows. Nowadays it's the children who are the ogres.'

'You're not doing much of a job at reassuring me.'

'Is it a guest's duty to report the doings of the family black sheep? What do the etiquette books say?'

'Mightn't the local police guide-to-survival be more useful?'

'Oh dear, a nervous guest. I'd better be careful. Did you know that nervousness causes three fourths of all fatal accidents? Relax. I made that up. Listen, I'm a serious fellow really. The chat is camouflage. I presume you came to this library for a book? Well, so did I. Look.' He handed her the one he had been holding. It was a snuff-brown volume with crumbling edges. 'A memoir by one of our ancestors who fought to save the last Florentine Republic in 1530. As I'm interested in what may be the last of the Italian Republic, I thought I'd check out analogies. Our ancestor was one of the *Arrabbiati*: men held in much the same esteem by conservatives then as my grandmamma holds today's activists.' His gap-toothed smile. He took a wallet from his shirt pocket, fished out a card and held it for her to see. It was his identity card. 'All right?' He put it back and waved at an armchair. 'Sit?'

They sat.

'I'm asking you,' he said, 'not to report me to my grandmamma – for *her* sake. I don't want her upset.'

They stared at each other for a challenging moment. 'How do I know,' Anne asked, 'that that would be right? There's so much I *don't* know . . .' She gestured at the flashlight.

'Ask Ida.'

'Did *she* let you in?' This – a shift of responsibility, would be reassuring.

'Not exactly.' He grinned. 'I have the keys of the house.' He swung them on his index finger. 'My mother let me have them. She's worried because she has quarrelled with Nonna Niccolosa. Over me, I'm afraid. Anyway, the upshot was that we've *both* been banished – which doesn't bother me since I disapprove of inherited wealth. Property is theft. But my mamma's beside herself. One does *not* leave a rich relative to die in the hands of ... outsiders. She hopes for a deathbed reconciliation. Has *la nonna* mentioned me by the way? What does she say?'

'She says,' Anne blurted, 'that if you were to be told a fairy story you'd want to know everyone's income.' She was shocked by the turn the talk had taken. Did this boy mean that *she* was the outsider against whom his grandmother needed defending? Perhaps he *hadn't* meant that? She mustn't be touchy. People here talked constantly about money and in the last few days she had got used to hearing the count and the marchesa spend half of every meal discussing property and expectations in a way which, at home, would be considered in terrible taste.

'Nonna Niccolosa said that?'

'Yes.'

'She knows her onions! She and I have a lot in common. Power and money interest us.' He rolled the words with relish. 'The difference is that I want to redistribute it and she doesn't.' Neri rose and danced about making scattering gestures. 'Don't worry, I'm not Robin Hood. I plan to redistribute it by political means. No theft. Do you believe that?'

'I've no reason not to.'

'And you'll do what I ask?' Putting a finger on his lips and tilting his head questioningly.

'Mightn't I,' she asked vengefully, 'be abusing your grand-mother's trust?'

'By not telling her I'd borrowed a book? Listen, how else was I to get it? It's very rare and she *has* banished me.'

'You could have asked Ida to get it.' There was a sound in the corridor. Was there? 'Does *she* know you're here?' Perhaps the step outside was Ida's.

'No, she doesn't.'

Anne made a silencing gesture. 'There's someone coming,' she heard herself warn.

Neri ducked behind a sofa.

'Anne,' called Niccolosa's voice. 'Are you in the library?' She appeared in the doorway. 'Is there someone with you? I thought I heard voices.'

'No, I was, um, reciting a poem to myself.'

'It sounded like two voices.'

'There *are* two,' Anne improvised. 'It's "The Owl and the Pussycat". I got a medal for reciting it when I was twelve.' A foot attached to a stretch of blue-denimed leg stuck round the end of the sofa. She backed towards it and gave it a discreet kick.

Niccolosa walked to the sofa and sat on it. Neri's foot was now out of her line of vision. 'I've been thinking,' she said. 'I kept thinking about you instead of getting to sleep, so in the end I decided to have a word with you and get it over. You won't mind if I'm frank?'

'That sounds ominous!' Anne felt a throb of awareness that *this* might be the conversation which the monsignor had suggested Niccolosa and she have about Mummy. They mustn't have it with Neri listening. How head it off?

'It's not that bad,' said Niccolosa, 'or rather the bad bit hasn't to do with you. It has to do with Guido.'

This was a different matter then. Anne began to feel anxious on another score.

'I'm afraid,' she heard, 'he's what used to be called "bad company" for a young girl.' The marchesa was clearly unstoppable. Her voice was urgent and she was frowning. 'Since *I* brought you together,' she said, 'I'm obviously responsible. I don't know how experienced you are with men, Anne? Not very, I expect. I'm thinking of older men, not students. Oddly – I suppose it sounds odd though, God knows, in my experience it's standard – older men are more irresponsible than young ones when it comes to women. They get nervous about their departing youth and lose all sense of – well, all sense. They become greedy, nervy and shameless. Guido, moreover, has never been scrupulous with women.' Niccolosa looked lengthily at Anne who, to her own annoyance, blushed.

'I hope this warning isn't going to have the wrong effect,' said Niccolosa. 'I don't want to make him sound a challenge and you mustn't think that I'm a kill-joy. I would like to think you believe me when I say that this talk is intended entirely for your benefit. It's nearly always the girl who gets hurt.' She sighed and was perhaps remembering Flavia.

Anne was flustered. 'I'm sorry if I've given you cause to worry.'

'It's not *you*, my dear.'

'Well ...'

Below and to one side of Niccolosa, Neri's foot did an ironic little dance in the air. Like a small puppet, it nodded its laced-up front in time to Niccolosa's affirmative remarks and shook itself when she made negative ones.

'Honestly ...' Anne began, then stopped.

The foot nodded unctuously.

'... nothing's happened.'

'I didn't think it had,' said Niccolosa, 'unless in your minds. I hope I'm not putting ideas *into* your minds. The trouble is that if I wait I may speak too late ...'

Nod, nod.

'... and if I don't ...'

Anne turned away from the foot. This meant that she was talking sideways to Niccolosa. 'I promise you nothing's happened. Nothing of any sort.'

'Have I upset you?' the old lady worried.

'No, no. I'm sorry your siesta was disturbed. Can I help you back up the stairs?' Sidling towards Niccolosa, Anne got a hand under her elbow, levered her from the couch and guided her to the library door.

Out in the corridor Ida appeared and took charge of her patient.

'You go back to the library,' Anne was told. 'Get on with your reading. Ida will look after me.'

Anne went back in and closed the door. 'The coast's clear.'

Neri crawled out. 'Well,' he grinned at her, 'what a surprise! You're a crack liar! Thanks. I'm grateful. *Are* you in love with my father?'

'No.'

'Why not? Why not?' Neri's movements were like a mime's – no, perhaps they were more like a puppy's: a release of energy and glee. 'Lots of women *have* been,' he told her. 'So, presumably, he's lovable as a lover. He's no good at all as a father. I'd have to warn you off him if you were looking for a father figure which, given your age difference, you might be. It would be unconscious of course. Let's see: what's your own father like? I'm rather up on all this, thanks to an American girl I had an affair with last summer. She ditched me because she decided she liked older men.'

'*My* father,' said Anne, intending this to put a damper on Neri, 'blew himself up with a bomb.'

'I'm sorry. Was he a revolutionary?'

'A soldier.'

'Well, I'm sorry anyway. How old were you when this happened?'

'Fifteen.'

'So you *may* be seeking a substitute. I can't stand my old man myself. Does he look like your father?'

'He does a bit.'

'Aha, and was your childhood unhappy?'

'A bit,' she repeated and wondered why she was letting this impertinent boy interrogate her. It was partly for the pleasure of hearing him talk about Guido. But his silliness soothed her too. Turning her feeling for Guido into something playful gave it shelter, made it safe from the spoiling blight with which her hostess had tried to contaminate it. However: 'You're cheeky, aren't you?' she felt she owed it to herself to say.

'Blame my unhappy childhood. I had one too: my father's fault. He was mainly an absentee and I preferred it that way. When he was around he was supercilious and unfair. My mother was no better. "Worldly" sums her up. Banal, isn't it? I suppose it's why I'm attracted to politics: the challenge to put their rotten world to rights. To be effective where they were triflers.'

'It's not an easy field to be effective in. Your grandmother favours farming.'

'Well she *would*! It's so moral and female! Plant seeds and reap the consequences. A conservative's dream, endlessly the same. My father's a natural conservative too. I used to have half an Oedipus complex: the part about killing him. But why bother to kill someone who's only half alive?

'He seems marvellously alive to me.'

'Oh dear, I'm afraid my grandmother's right. You'll have to be rescued. He's a shadow really: all contingent and adaptable. He's been finding loopholes in the law for so long that he no longer believes in right and wrong. For him *everything* is dependent on something else. Ask my father if it's wrong to lie to the tax authorities about one's income. "No," he will tell you with assurance, for he once took the question to a theologian who belongs to his party. "No," he'll say, "it's not wrong since the Italian tax authorities automatically assume that I will lie. Therefore, *if* I tell the truth, they will double the figure I give them and tax me on that. Since I actually told the truth, the figure they arrive at is false and thus I have contributed to their deceiving themselves as well as cheating myself and my family. *Thus*, here in Italy, the only way to truth is through lies. QED." '

Anne laughed. 'It could be true.'

'But that's what's so cynical! Accepting the situation and adapting to it. Decades of doing that got us where we are. Centuries even! Why do you defend him?'

'How earnest you are all of a sudden!' Anne was now the teasing one. 'Maybe I defend him because you attack him.'

'I have to,' said Neri. 'He's so charming. My mother is too: *simpatica* and so forth. That's why I never had the other half of the Oedipus complex for even a minute. One couldn't fantasize about marrying someone like that. One would want something fated and inevitable. I would anyway. I detect frivolous tendencies in myself. I need weighting down. Maybe *you're* my fate? I like your being a bit priggish. Don't be offended. We seem to have a lot in common.'

'I think I'd pick your father over you.'

'Ha! Now maybe I'll start wanting to kill him again.'

'I imagine killers talk less.'

'Yes. Well. Killing doesn't really appeal to me. I don't want to give you the wrong impression. I don't think I've thought of it seriously since I was twelve. It's become banal around here since Sardinian kidnappers moved into Tuscany. A nasty lot. They feed their victims to their pigs – which might be the origin of the myth of Circe, don't you think? Turning people into swine? There's something primitive and dark about them: inbred monsters from that ancient island. That's one of the frightening results of moving populations about. It releases pre-rational forces. Delivers them on your doorstep. Circe and the Cyclops appear in the land of reason and reason cannot comprehend them. I'm not for political violence either. It ends up serving the purposes of the police. There are people who think they can harness the forces of Cyclops and Circe, but they find the harness broken and horror on the loose.

Violence is either egomania or else it's manipulated. People like my father . . .'

'You can't mean *he's* a man of violence?'

'It's all related, dear girl. He's not violent but thinks he can handle the violent men by deals and skill. You can't. It only encourages them. Cyclops doesn't understand deals. I'm talking of the government of this wretched country – lovely country. I love my country, but it's in the wrong hands. The sins of the fathers are secret and we suffer for them.'

'Of *your* father?'

'Of mine and others. He who beds down with dogs, they say, gets up with fleas. My father must feel the odd itch. I must go. Killing – remember I say so – is *not* an impressive act.'

'What is?'

'Saving someone from being killed maybe. I'm off. Are we agreed?'

'I'll keep my mouth shut.'

'Thanks.' He opened the shutter, slid out, closed it and was gone.

Back in her room, Anne chewed over the implications of her chat with Neri, concentrating on the ones concerning herself. Much of what he'd said struck her as froth. He was only two calendar years younger than she but was, she had decided, decades younger emotionally. She had met boys like that at the university: cunning, bookish, bright, they used their wits to keep the real world at bay and risked staying childish until they grew old enough to be considered eccentric. Girls rarely got away with that. Such people could have insights though, and she worried lest he really believed her to be after 'power and money'. Ingratiating herself with his grandmother even? The thought was horrid and hadn't entered her mind. Could she have been doing it unknowingly?

No. Yet, how totally shake a suspicion like that? Besides, the idea now *was* in her mind: dark, poisonous and spreading. The way to shake it would be to leave – which would mean she would never see Guido again. Not that much was likely to come of her seeing him. But the relinquishing mood was one she had primed herself to check. Halt! Watch it, Anne! Don't do what Mummy did with Cosimo. Ever. Not for one split second must you follow *her* sad libretto and back away from hope, bowing as if it were royalty. No, you stick around and give a chance to luck and love. Yes: love. Have a bit of nerve.

This morning Ida had washed the marchesa's hair. She handled the tender scalp delicately, running her fingers through the brittle strands softened by conditioner so as to loosen knots and tangles, then rinsing and towelling with a deftness developed for dealing with baby chickens, calves and young plants. Ida had been raised on a farm. While doing this, she went into an alert dream, a sort of self-hypnosis which kept the needed faculties awake while inducing an agreeable semi-sleep in the rest of her mind and body. She was never im-patient. She enjoyed this state which came on her unbidden and was perhaps inherited from generations of country people for whom monotony and wariness were the conditions of survival.

The marchesa shook her out of it.

Just when Ida had got her comfortably backed up against her pillows, smelling pleasantly of shampoo, she began to rail and take on.

'Well, that's done,' Ida had said with satisfaction.

'Done!' groaned the invalid in an ululation of anguish. 'Done why? For what? For how long?' If every move was to be an effort and a pain, why make it? Living, she groaned, was one long round of drudgery, though she hadn't acknowledged this fully until now. You didn't in your youth. Then animal energy carried and blinded you so that you rushed about and arranged and managed and ate and defecated and washed and married and procreated creatures who would do the same. Why? Could Ida tell her? *Why?* To exist? Why want to? If there was a God, why did *he* want to? Energy was all there was: appetites, a self-perpetuating cycle and for what?

Niccolosa was exhausted. Ida wiped her chin and left her staring at the ceiling while her jaw fell open and now and then her teeth gnashed. With her damp frill of white hair combed back from her face, she bore a faint resemblance to a fish. Poor marchesa! Poor soul!

Ida began to think of calling in a new doctor. But who? The 'P' page of the marchesa's address book had had to be replaced because of the number of *professori* from the great hospitals of Florence, Rome and Milan whom she had consulted and whose advice she had chosen to ignore. They had wanted her to go into their hospitals, saying that they wouldn't be responsible for what might happen if she didn't. But she had said that what would happen, no matter what, was that she would die. Then, one after the other, she had crossed the names of the great *professori* out of her address book.

Ida's feelings about resignation had vanished. Defiance animated her. She was focused on her purpose which was to communicate the life current to her patient. Anxiously, she soothed and rallied, hovered, tucked in and tried to coax the marchesa from her apathy. When the marchesa asked for a weak cup of herbal tea, Ida complied with the request, but scrutinized it too, like a farmer scrutinizing the weather. Any appetite was hopeful – but what of the words 'weak' and 'little'? They minimized the trouble to which Ida was being put, the patient's appetite and perhaps her tantrum of just now. They came close to wheedling – and that had never been the Signora Marchesa's style.

When Ida brought up a pot of fresh verbena tisane, the

invalid did, however, perk up a little, sniffing the fragrance and saying that it reminded her of the stretch of kitchen-garden where the verbena tree grew.

'That wouldn't happen if I were in hospital,' she said. 'The imagination fails. It can only travel so far.' Drinking her tisane, she asked, 'How are the scented stock this year?'

'Lovely. Will I pick you some?'

'No, thank you, no. The verbena is enough.'

Ida decided to phone the Signor Marchese in Rome and let him decide what to do. This forgoing and doing without was not a good sign at all.

The monsignor found Anne sunbathing on the terrace and paused for a chat.

'Please,' he insisted. 'Don't move. I don't want to disturb you.'

He sounded so anxious about this that it seemed polite to stay put even though she had begun to feel uncomfortably hot and removing the eye-mask from her eyes made everything dazzle. Had he perhaps meant for her to keep *that* on too? She held it doubtfully in her hand but thought, no, it would be rude to put it back. It would be as though she didn't want to see him. Actually, she couldn't anyway. With the sun in her eyes, he was a black blob shimmering at the edges like a spreading hole. She couldn't concentrate on what he was saying. It was to do with a talk he'd had with the marchesa who struck him as having taken a turn for the worse. The one thing cheering her was satisfaction at having spoken to Anne.

'Really?'

'*You're* not too upset, I hope?' He hadn't, he said, had a chance to ask the marchesa how Anne had taken things. She was too ill and Ida had more or less chased him out of the sickroom. He laughed at this. 'Was it a shock?' he asked solicitously.

'No.'

'Maybe you'd rather not discuss it just yet?'

Anne couldn't see what there was to discuss. Really, it was too bad of Niccolosa to go telling tales and making mountains out of molehills. She wished the monsignor would sit down. He kept looming over her, looking, with the sun on him, like a great, gold-rimmed, furry bumble bee.

'That's right. I'd rather not.'

That seemed to disappoint him, but he began to talk of something else. His tone veered from the preachy to the gossipy, as though changing ecclesiastical mores had left him unsure which to adopt. He was prone to lunges of frankness.

'Better say nothing to Guido,' he advised.

Anne was too hot to blush.

'Don't get up,' he begged. 'Please. I didn't want to spoil your sunbath.'

'I was getting too hot.' She moved into the shade and looked straight at him.

By now, however, he had lapsed into small talk, piloting it from architecture – this villa – to the common illusion that the past was more ordered and elegant than our own day. That, he surmised, came from so many listed buildings being preserved. 'They, you see, would have been the best and quite untypical. Meanwhile the jerrybuilt stuff got cleared away with all the other mistakes and messes of life. If anything,' he said, 'the past was harder to live in. You must be understanding. A high-spirited, generous girl like your mother could slip from sheer innocence into the sort of trap which the cynical would evade.'

Anne supposed she must have missed some connection. Perhaps he was talking about Cosimo, though she hadn't thought anyone, apart from Guido, knew about that.

'It's only a generation back,' said the monsignor, 'but so much has changed. The need for secrecy may seem hypocritical to a young person of your generation. But facing the music was often unthinkable then. Scandal was considered the worst sin. Your mother did try to brave it out at the beginning. When she went to live in her little love-nest in Florence . . .'

Anne interrupted him: 'I think I ought to tell you that I don't understand a word you've said. What love-nest? Are you telling me that my mother was carrying on with Cosimo *before* he came to Dublin?'

'Cosimo?'

'There wasn't anyone else, was there? What year are you talking about?'

'You mean . . .' The monsignor crumpled. 'The marchesa didn't . . . *Oddio!* You don't know?'

'Know what? I know that my mother had an affair in Dublin with a man called Cosimo. That was after her marriage. I've been wanting to find out about him but nobody seems to know who he was. Do you?'

'Oh, my dear . . . So the marchesa . . . ?'

'What about her? I've asked *her* about Cosimo, but she doesn't know of him. Do you?'

'No.'

'But you seem to know a lot. What was this about a love-nest in Florence?'

But the monsignor, plucking at his garments like an itchy crow, had withdrawn into amnesia and inarticulateness. One statement emerged like the crow's caw: he had never heard of Cosimo. Cosimo? Never heard the name. '*Mai,*' he cawed and multiplied pleas that Anne not judge anyone. *Caritas* and comprehension were invoked.

'So with whom did she have a love-nest in Florence?'

'I can't tell you. She left here and the marchesa thought she was in Dublin with her parents while her parents thought she was at the villa. Naturally, in the end, the thing came out. There were telegrams to the Irish embassy. A small scandal.

The marchesa said she had talked to you. I supposed it was about this. I can't tell you any more. Wait until she's feeling better. She's too weak today.'

'Well,' said Anne, 'I don't suppose any of it matters much now.' Though, of course, she reflected, everything old and past did matter to these people. The villa was like an old people's home. Memories worked best with the long ago, and belonging to the past was a recommendation in itself. Indeed, her own claim to Niccolosa's attention was entirely through Mummy.

'I'd better go,' said the monsignor. 'I'm sorry if I've upset you. Sorry. Sorry.'

Deprecating and fidgety, a noonday shadow, he retreated from the terrace and down the dusty drive: a squat figure, pausing from time to time to wipe his forehead with a large, blue handkerchief. The cypresses towering above him were as black as he but stood utterly immobile in the windless heat. Their plumes were as compact as bearskins and, according to the marchesa, were five hundred years old.

Property, it struck Anne, must have been the head and tail of Mummy's story and of Flavia's too. One had it, one hadn't, and each was expected to mate accordingly, renouncing all impulse. If bred to renunciation, how break step? At a plunge? Flavia must have been the plunging sort. In and out of beds, Anne surmised, until the ultimate plunge down that final cold crevasse. RIP Flavia. There had been people in that generation who walked about as though they had a time-bomb in their genitals.

Mummy had probably not plunged enough. What had the monsignor meant by 'hypocritical' and 'not facing the music'? Did he mean that she had married Daddy on the rebound? Probably. And yet it now looked as if she had shown more spirit than Anne had ever supposed. Poor Mummy! Poor yearner! It made Anne feel closer to her to know that she had tried to follow her dream and actually gone to live in what the monsignor so quaintly and diminishingly called a 'love-nest'. Maybe Mummy had been braver then than Anne had imagined? Maybe she had simply had no luck?

Or no money? Very likely *that* had been the handicap. An *au pair* didn't tend to have it and Florentines gave it importance. It figured big in their vocabulary. *Grana, danaro, soldi.* For all Anne knew, they had as many words for it as Eskimos did for snow. It wouldn't surprise her. Their name, after all, was related to the name of a coin.

Niccolosa had recommended that Anne read the letters of Alessandra Strozzi (1407–71), a brisk woman who, while her male relatives were under political ban, had run their estates, farmed, arranged marriages and – by means of these letters – kept the exiles minutely and dutifully informed.

Property had been pivotal to the Strozzis, as to all Florentines, a merchant people whose domestic architecture had the gridlike simplicity of a bank vault. Even Neri seemed to keep it in the forefront of his mind, and Anne felt that these five-hundred-year-old letters explained a lot about her hosts. Well, that was probably part of Niccolosa's plan. She seemed intent on completing Anne's education.

Thrift and the taboos which keep passion from disrupting long-term plans ran like red lines in a cashbook through Alessandra's letters. Marriage, in her book, was a commercial transaction.

Odd that Mummy herself should have failed to get to the bottom line. Never in years of langorous chat had she shown any sign of knowing what underpinned the rules governing nice girls' conduct, fuelled the plots of her favourite operas and must in the end have prevented her following her heart:

Soldi, danaro, fiorini, grana, a jingling refrain.

Why hadn't she gone off with bloody Cosimo?

Soldi, etc.

Why, thought Anne irritably, do I care about that stupid

woman who happened to give birth to me? She groaned with
fury for her mother but more for her father and herself who,
like contiguous ninepins, had staggered beneath the blow
which felled *her*. For years she was a sour nag to poor Dad
who never knew why his pretty wife was for ever picking on
him, laughed at his rank and compared the Irish army to the
Swiss navy. How could he? Her confidences were all for Anne
who first heard of Cosimo about the same time as she heard
of Little Boy Blue. Daddy excluded from the story-telling
sessions and made to feel inadequate for reasons unspecified,
gave up trying to understand and, when at the end of his
tether, would volunteer to do some more bomb-defusing.

Poor Daddy!

After years of pity for this rueful shadow which had hovered
out of reach of her mother's irritation, Anne still found herself
conjuring away anxiety with that exclamation. Perhaps everyone had such filler phrases? Italians said '*Mamma mia*'. A
memory of the Madonna, *that* called on a fount of strength.
'Poor Daddy' was more of a *miserere*, more of a groan for
the downtrodden first recognized in her father's fuzzy, honey-
coloured, well-meaning face.

Poor Daddy! *Mamma mia!* Neri was wrong in his speculations about Anne. She was not looking for a father figure.
She wanted what her mother had wanted and failed to hold
on to: a fiery, thrilling love with a happy ending. Poor Daddy,
poor Mummy! Anne did not intend ending like either of them.

Her interest in Cosimo was purely antiquarian.

'Did you know a man called Cosimo?' she had asked
Niccolosa some days ago.

'Cosimo?' Niccolosa thought for a while that perhaps she
did but, on reflection, realized that it had been the name,
not of a man, but of several horses owned and bred by
Bonaccorso: Cosimo, Cosimino, Coco the Third.

*

'Will you let me give you a pair of ear-rings?' Niccolosa asked Anne. 'I don't wear them. Pendants and bits and bobs look terrible on old ladies. Too many old dears look like birds. They moult. Or like cheap statues of the Virgin in country parishes with offerings pinned all over them. On *you* these will look very nice.'

They were coral and gold.

'Very nice,' approved Niccolosa. 'You dress too severely. Wear them this evening. You know it cheers me immensely to have you here. You've no idea. I regretted that your mother never came back. Really. I wrote and invited her but she never came.'

'She was ill,' said Anne. 'She was ill for years.'

'That's no reason. Lots of sick people come to our spas. She could have come to Montecatini. It would have done her a world of good.'

'It wasn't that sort of illness.'

'Spas are for *fun*! They're good for any illness. They cheer people up. Give them a lift. She lacked nerve, you know,' said Niccolosa. 'Was she a bad patient?'

'Yes.'

'I guessed that. It's why *you're* such a good nurse. It's how you learned to be so sweet and patient. Wear the ear-rings tonight. I'm coming down to dinner if it kills me.'

Anne had fallen asleep over the memoirs of yet another of Niccolosa's ancestors, a dashing figure who had travelled fifteenth-century Europe trading horses, jewels, wine and saffron, gambling and making loans to warring kings and captains. In her dream he merged with Guido with whom Anne was now in love. Neither Niccolosa's warning, her effort – if that was what it was – to buy Anne off with the gift of ear-rings, nor Guido's silence was a dissuasion. In Anne's mind he loved her back. Her feeling guaranteed his. It was a magnetism whose current held them both, and it was her sense of this which had made the lines of print tilt and send her into a trance which was not far removed from her waking state. Focused and intent, she was no longer anxious. All she need do was wait – unless her conviction was mere dream? Dreaming, she debated this, wondering whether to wake up. The figure who was both Guido and his ancestor was rolling dice with French gamblers.

'Be careful!'

The setting was sinister and the other players had the sly, puffed faces of cardsharpers in paintings by George de la Tour. A candle flickered. A dagger glinted.

'Look out!'

The gambler threw his dice.

Someone blew out the candle – she felt breath hot on her cheek. There was darkness; a table overturned and ... She screamed and woke up.

Guido Cavalcanti's face was within inches of her own which he was intently scrutinizing. They were on the terrace and the gambler's memoirs had fallen on the ground. Sunset. Down below bats pulsed in a sediment of twilight. Fragmented as in a kaleidoscope, reality was vivid but shifty.

'I was thinking of kissing you.'

'Why didn't you?'

He kissed her. Another kind of trance. Timeless. Thrilling. Then they came back to time. She hugged him.

'I wish I were a boa-constrictor. Then I'd cripple and hold you for ever.'

Precariousness gave edge to her joy. Absent, she had been sure of him. Now that he was here, she became miserly and doubtful, calculating and wondering how much of him she held in her arms. His son and mother thought him a philanderer and a fly-by-night seducer.

'Tell me . . .' But she could hardly start so soon to interrogate him. 'Am I awake?' she asked instead.

'Yes, Sleeping Beauty. Did you need a spell broken?'

'No. No, I want the spell, only I want you under it too. Your mother said . . .'

'Ah, you've been discussing me!' He was amused, frivolous – a philanderer?

'When you looked at me,' she forced herself to ask, 'in that way you have . . . just now and the other evening too . . . What did it mean?'

'Did I frighten you? What a shy mouse it is!' He was running his fingers over her features. Light, delicate fingers. Attentive – but was this like the attentiveness of someone taking a brass rubbing? Skilled? Detached?

'I was seeing your mother in you. My youth. It was a shock. I'm sorry if I stared. But the cancelling of twenty-five years can knock one off stroke.'

'So that was all?' Her body felt like lead. It fell, collapsing into itself, yet seemed to be still upright and still suffering the sensation of falling.

'All?' He kissed her. It was a quick, hushing little kiss. 'Don't say "all" as if all were nothing. It's a breath-taking phenomenon: the fallen blossom blooms afresh on the branch. A miracle. You're too young to know what I'm talking about. You provoke the sensation but can't feel it.' He combed his fingers through her hair, bunched it at her neck and held her head at arm's length. ' "Fair is youth and void of sorrow," ' he quoted. ' "Yet it hourly flies away!" And then flies back and looks reproachfully at me. Why the reproach, *bambina*? That's a rotten translation, by the way. Originals are always better.'

'Like my mother?'

'Flirt!' He gave her a cheerful squeeze. 'Let's go in before the mosquitoes devour us.'

Humming the song like a great frolicsome bee: hmmm hm hmmm, he propelled her ahead of him. Anne, though ready to melt, remembered an old determination never to be a man's plaything, nor engage – if in love herself – with less than all of him. But suppose his heart were inaccessible? Wouldn't it be the loneliest of fates to find yourself gravely in love – at last, Anne! – with someone who had lost touch with his own deep feelings? Were men of Guido's age necessarily mean in their commitments?

CHAPTER FOUR

Bonaccorso was keyed up. Cosa – he was the last one left to call her that – was dining downstairs for the first time in three days and the doctor had been evasive about the outlook. Tonight Guido was here from Rome and the girl too was at dinner, wearing a pair of Cosa's ear-rings. The sight of them gave Bonaccorso a twinge. They had been a small gift from himself made, what, oh, maybe forty years ago, to commemorate a christening at which Cosa and he had been godparents. She must have forgotten. She had a lot to distract her, whereas he remembered everything – well, a lot: Cosa wearing those ear-rings; Cosa as a young mother surrounded with babies – two had died of scarlet fever; Cosa wearing a driving veil, laughing through it, teasing him and saying that his horses were his true family and his incestuous breeding pattern – he had been trying to isolate the best features of the strain, hoping for a fleet, strong racer – was 'utterly typical'. Meaning, he supposed, of him and of his dry, theoretical approach. Odd to remember that he had once been thought 'a brain' and 'promising'. Well, the promise had not been kept. She must have meant too that it was typical of his absoluteness – like his refusal to marry once *she* had turned him down. 'Funny old Bobo!' He had *had* to be a joke. It was either that or a threat. He had agreed to the tacit bargain and, thereafter, for half a century, dined at least once a week with the Cavalcantis, enjoying family life at second hand. He had asked her to marry him when he was nineteen – too young according to her family, who thought him unstable. Like his horses – which had had to be auctioned off – his stock, though good, was erratic. So he became a sort of honorary brother to her and now, looking back, couldn't honestly say that it hadn't been for the best. He liked getting back to his congenial house after an evening's conviviality. It was a caricature of an English one, furnished with mahogany and dark clutter by a homesick English grand-mother and utterly un-Tuscan – like the horse-breeding venture undertaken in defiance of draught and local wisdom. He had never been to England. Odd: his life could be defined by negatives. Never had children, never made love to a woman of his class nor worked for any man but himself. It had not, he considered, been unhappy. Cosa said he hadn't wanted the things he didn't get. Maybe.

'So you never visited the British Isles?' The girl, following Cosa's lead, was teasing him. He was a man whom women teased. A bachelor landowner fell into the teasable category the minute he fell out of the marriageable one. 'Why ever not?' It was her voice that teased. The question was a fair one. She smiled, he had to admit, enchantingly. She was a pretty creature. Good for Cosa. Young life. Peasants believed the old could suck it from the young. There were some quite gross stories – well, never mind. Mere propinquity was good. He had thought of offering Cosa a puppy. The girl would be less trouble.

Why not? He had wondered himself, most frequently in the mornings before his shaving mirror, holding conversations with it as he cut swathes in the lather with his razor. One could get narcissistic. Sometimes, checking this, he recited virile verses learned from Nanny Doyle. 'How can man die better,' for instance, 'than facing fearful odds/For the ashes of his fathers/And the temples of his gods?' Tumta tumta.

Rousing stuff. Though, for perfectly honourable reasons, he hadn't been in the army, he enjoyed martial verse. 'Admit old chap,' he sometimes told his pink-slashed image, 'that it's odd you never went, given your English tastes and faultless grasp of the language!' Friends from the local English colony had assured him of its faultlessness. It was perhaps a trifle old-fashioned. Dialogue in recent films perplexed him though he had tried to keep up, reading *The Times* when he remembered to buy it and ordering his shirts from Harvey and Hudson. Englishness had been a passion which it was too late now to consummate. He was rheumaticky and the climate would not do for him. Too late to shoot grouse or fish salmon. If he had gone years ago he might even have done some fox-hunting. 'If wishes were horses, beggars might ride.' Not quite what he meant but he liked the blunt brutality of the proverb. Straight from the shoulder. 'When Adam delved, and Eve span/Who was then a gentleman?' Subversive, that one. But – English people of good class assured him – their system was still so secure that freedoms which might turn other societies topsy-turvy could be tolerated with non-chalance. Not here. Here you had to hold the pass. 'Then spake the brave Horatio/The keeper of the gate/"To every man upon this earth/Death cometh soon or late ..."' Was it coming now to Cosa? He hoped not. He couldn't *think* of life without her. Never made love to her. Hadn't even pushed very hard to be considered when she became a widow – years ago now – but she filled his life. Shaped it. Simple as that. Her style. Her nerve. Their joint memories. Habit, if you liked to say so – but then be fair and say it also of the most uxorious of marriages and most passionate of love affairs. The bonds could only be severed by radical surgery. Like Siamese twins. You read of cases where they shared a heart. Sometimes, he'd felt he shared one with Cosa. She mightn't agree. Perhaps the heart was more his, more on his side of their joint astral body? Nonsense. Must be getting eccentric. Wasn't – though he might have done so without her.

The reason he'd never gone to England was that when young he hadn't the cash and later it was too late. First his father had taken so long to die and then the farm had had to be made to pay. To be sure, the young now travelled on a shoestring but he, wanting to be a nabob, couldn't have borne imperfection. So who was the more passionate pilgrim? If you dreamed of visiting Rome, you didn't want to arrive like a Goth. Backpacking, my God. Sleeping in parks!

He would have liked to discuss this with the company, but talk had got on to some other track. Someone – the girl, was it? – was saying that the first rule of life was to go after what you wanted and win.

'A bit crude surely?' Guido demurred. 'Primitive even. What about the notion that the last shall be first and losers win?'

'They may do in heaven,' shrugged the girl, 'but access to that is dicey and, for all we know, the ruthless and pushy may be first there too.'

Bonaccorso was amused. The spring lamb mouths cynicism, while the wolf quotes the Sermon on the Mount.

'Might the message,' Guido wondered, 'refer less to heaven than to how we live in our minds?'

'We make our own paradise?'

'Why not?'

Bonaccorso tittered. Seduction was a good spectator sport.

'Why not,' the girl agreed, 'though the outer world does impinge.'

And does, Bonaccorso reflected with a tilt of mood, with-draw. Like Cosa. By now she was mostly a creature of his mind. How dependent was he on her real presence? Even when he was with her, he saw several simultaneous images:

the young Cosa, an ideal Cosa, the woman actually there. Did he need *that* one? He did. He did. Memory, a wispy thing, would not sustain him. It would not survive.

Guido and the girl were arguing and sparring: a process which had gone on between himself and Cosa for, oh, more years than he wanted to put a number to. So abraded by it were their two personalities that they fitted now as smoothly as bolt and socket. Yes, if they fought now it was more by way of a reminder, a nudging back to when the rows were real and hot with hurt – oh, it had probably never been anything but a venting of animal energy, that excessive, explosive energy of youth. Good to be past that. The girl was boiling with it. You could *see* and feel it. Heat flew from her like sparks from a tinder.

It was affecting Cosa. All feverish attention, she kept crumbling bread without eating it and lifting an empty wine glass to her lips. She had refused a refill. Bonaccorso saw that she minded Guido's attempts with the girl. Why? People did what they chose. Each to his taste. Sex, in his view, was mostly a substitute for intimacy and tenderness. In his own life he'd kept them apart. Honester. He did see though that dishonesty, the mix of unmixables, brought excitements which neither he nor his stud stallions were likely to know. 'Love ever to the gentle heart repairs!' Such bosh! Delusions! Were they more defensible than those procured by drugs? Well, possibly in the case of Dante, Petrarch and Co. Not that he'd read *them* since his schooldays. But their work was one of the prides of Tuscany and quotations engraved on calendars, ash trays and inside one's own head had perhaps had their effect.

'Curious,' it came back to him and he told the company: 'this villa was the setting for a sixteenth-century dialogue on love. Such debates were all the rage then: a parlour game. Platonic love mostly – that made it decent – would be discussed by youths and maidens, then written up by some humanist.'

'Love?' Cosa glared as though *he'd* introduced the subject.

'A poet's game,' he apologized. 'No doubt often a substitute.'

'For *what*?'

He'd annoyed her. This addled his wits. Words, anyway, came less readily now. Sometimes one said anything at all simply to fill a silence. Babbled or lapsed into another tongue. Each had its speciality. The Emperor Charles V had advised speaking Spanish to God, French to one's mistress and – what? Bonaccorso's head was a sieve. 'Whoo!' he produced the indrawn whistle he used with his pet canaries. 'Whoo!' Growing old was like evolution in reverse. He'd reached the bird stage. Out in the garden an owl, as though to mock him, cried *kyu, kyu, kyu.*

'I remember those dialogues,' said Guido. 'They posed questions like "Is the lover rendered nobler by love? Is he a better citizen?" Conclusions were usually favourable.'

'That,' said his mother, 'was because the humanists were thinking of God who the priests had told them *was* love. I've never seen why. If he *were* and we made in his image, there should be more evidence for it. Instead, all I see around is sex. Demographic explosions.' She frowned. 'Is God a sort of Easter Bunny?'

'Surely love,' Bonaccorso made an effort to pull his thoughts together, 'the ideal of it, knowing it exists, makes life tolerable?' He had an impulse to whistle again in celebration of the clarity of that.

'Well, given the meanness of the actual act,' said Niccolosa, 'it certainly needs idealizing. I suppose you imply that the ennobling rhetoric can spill over and ennoble everything else?'

Guido took her up on this. 'In Florence,' he claimed, 'that rhetoric was stolen from religion: a theft as important in its way as Prometheus's theft of fire. What had been God's was applied to man who could now become a sort of god. This had tremendous implications. You had to merit godliness – work your way up. Your lady was a God-appointed umpire who assessed your progress. Later she became a God-substitute. Paradise here with her was a foretaste of heaven. The ordinary burgher was thus given a way to the ineffable and high-flung which had once been the preserve of priests and princes.'

Bonaccorso giggled. 'Ineffable effing.'

'A magician's bag of tricks then?' asked the girl. 'All things to all men?'

'And only to men!' approved Cosa. 'It was a purely masculine rhetoric. Women – you read this in the old manuals of conduct – were advised to resist its blandishments.'

'But those manuals,' Guido objected, 'were written by men too. Fathers and husbands put them in women's hands. Lovers slipped them the poems and dialogues.'

'Counter-arguments of thieves and householders then?'

'Really, Mamma, if this is what reading the memoirs of our money-grubbing ancestors does for you, you should stop.'

'They,' said his mother, 'built the city of Florence and this villa and needed no metaphors. Your poets were either social failures who had to invent imaginary systems to justify themselves or lick-spittles who wrote to exalt some patron's prowess in the bedroom.'

'So the noblest activity of man is to keep his nose in the till?'

'Prove to me that it is love-making.'

'A challenge, Mamma?'

'If you like to take it that way.'

'*Bene!*' said Guido. 'Listen then, the three of you. If I convince you, you may give me what you like. If not, *I'll* give *you* a magnum of vintage champagne. Taitinger, Heidsieck, Veuve Cliquot. Choose your mark.'

'Done!' said Bonaccorso greedily. He liked a good champagne.

Guido raised his glass. 'Let's start with the tendency of species to put forth their best specimens at mating time – in certain herds the males fight for the privilege – and of each specimen to put forth its best features so as to attract the best mate and reproduce the best progeny for the herd. Unconsciously, this sense of mission takes over. Exhilaration grips the participants. Humans call it "love". It's a sense of sharing in something which goes beyond the self or the pair. For materialists it is the only self-transcendence.'

'All you're saying,' said his mother, keeping score, 'is that you, Guido, know no other form of self-transcendence. But *anything* which shakes us from our groove can produce that feeling. The approach of death does it. Ultimate freedom for the will is when the will can do nothing. There's a kind of glee in being helpless.'

Bonaccorso thought: 'She's getting ready to die. She won't struggle.' Resentment crawled through him.

'No,' Guido rebutted. 'There's more to it than that. Sexual passion excludes all for the good of all – thence the notion of the lover as self-absorbed or mad. It focuses him, but through him the species is seeking its interest.'

'Well then ...'

'Wait. As the species – or, in larger terms, Nature – uses the lovers, it also endows them with its resources: cosmic excitement and a sense of magnitude which transcends their ordinary selves. This is only fair since they are about Nature's work. Thus each sees in the other, at that moment, the power and firstness of creation. Each, briefly, becomes divine.'

'An illusion then?'

'Yes, but also: no. Because like any forceful drive, this

one magnetizes other forces. The powerful male gets the best mate. Then the notion of power becomes isolated in the minds of the contenders. For a thinking species like ours, sex thus leads to *thoughts* about power, property, beauty, loss and the notion of justice starting with the question: who deserves the best mate and why? All concerns are magnetized towards this one because it is not only basic, powerful and necessary but conflictual too, since the creature at the apex of health, power, etc. begins to surrender all these gifts to the next generation.'

'Whoo!' whistled Bonaccorso. '*Tristitia!* Tragedy.'

'While saying "love",' observed Niccolosa, 'you've been talking about nothing but sex. You *do* think God is the Easter Bunny! Love is durable, the sexual peak brief and your claim for the one can't be extended to the other.'

'They connect,' said Guido. 'Durability is the triumph of society over Nature – or, if you like, of Nature transforming itself by social means. The flashpoint passes but its memory links the couple. Given a bit of social encouragement, what better forger of links? Ecstasy: the furnace of pleasure.'

'And what of those who want repeated ecstasies and to turn the flashpoint into a conflagration?'

'*Mandrilli!* Satyrs! Probably they don't love at all in the sense I've been describing. Extremity is not willingly faced over and over. Real love is serious. It alerts and expands. It is the race at its height and the couple through which it works sees with peeled, visionary eyes.'

'Chosen ones only then?'

'They choose each other.'

'But are an élite?'

'Not in our society.' Guido poured himself some more wine. 'In our society what they get is social *dis*couragement. Hence all the sad songs.'

'So love is a weak force? I think you owe us some champagne.'

'Oh,' said Guido, 'you prick me on. I've been trying to talk with the spirit of those sixteenth-century debaters. It's hard to do. The vocabulary has got devalued. Words like "élite". Remember this rhetoric came from religion and I was trying to show that love is *noble*. If I go on you must imagine I'm telling a fairy story and treat the words accordingly. Give them back their innocence and wholeness. All right?'

'All right.'

'Well, they're an élite then, *but* man-become-god in the creative act represents collective interests. It is about this sort of love that poets write in vocabularies drawn from whatever discipline seems major at the time. Their heightened consciousness – as poets in and on love – makes them look afresh on all concerns. It's only when they misuse the same language to discuss lust that nausea ensues. Nothing wrong with lust, mind. It's quick and cheerful, but the Puritan feels a need to promote it a bit since he dislikes admitting to a "mere" appetite. It's from this lying promotion that *tristitia* comes – awareness of a hoax and cheat – and not, I think, from the pain of knowing that sex links with death. *That* can enhance the joy when the love is strong.'

'You've turned love into a sort of morality.'

'Yes.'

'So God is love?'

'No. Man can be god, an old Florentine heresy and a lot finer to my mind than the Jewish notion of God becoming man to be humiliated and sacrificed. My case rests.'

Bonaccorso had been disagreeably moved. The notion of the species at its height reproached. One should have had children: a civic duty especially when one's family was old, illustrious and in danger of dying out and populations everywhere becoming bastardized. Yes, yes. Now his sisters' sons would have to take the name. Well, he wasn't a breeder. Maybe Nature had decided against him and given him weak urges? Maybe. Maybe his horse-breeding had been some sort of surrogate? Fuck? Our horses can do that for us! He tittered. The others gave him odd looks. Whoo!

The girl asked some question about the risks of mistaking the mating dance for the deep movements of a partner's soul. Well, well, those two were well away. Bonaccorso felt the ghost of an urge. If he were in town tonight, he might ... No, no. Those little things on the Florentine streets could be riddled with disease. He had a safe connection in Milan – but going *there* involved forethought. Guido was saying that there must be risks in any worthwhile activity. Caution, he argued, and the conserving backwater life brought decadence. Bonaccorso felt got at. He *was* a passionate man. Did they think him a prudent, slippered old bachelor? He was passionate, it seemed to him, as a monk is passionate: fastidious, selective and uncompromising. He made and lived by distinctions. They, on the other hand, followed their appetites, then celebrated and rationalized them. All that spew Guido had tossed forth was nothing but a mating song. Aimed at the girl. Lots of bosh. Bonaccorso pitied the human race if it was to be reproduced uniquely by the likes of them. But it was notorious – just read the papers! – that the least discriminating elements in society had the highest reproduction rate. That had been perfectly all right, in fact useful, when such people were needed for labour as serfs and slaves. Now they were out of control. They were the new Goths.

Even if Bonaccorso and his like had had ten children apiece they could not have held the pass. They might not have tried. Look at Guido's son. Guido should talk. *He* had produced a puny specimen.

But Bonaccorso felt belittled and defiled. Obscurely – and so unanswerably – his life had been put on trial.

When Guido asked if his motion had been carried, Bonaccorso dissented firmly. Let him get his reward from the girl and give them their champagne. Brut, Bonaccorso wanted, Heidsieck. Cosa dissented too and the girl, since her vote would now make no difference, said neither aye nor nay.

'You didn't vote,' said Guido.

'Oh, I was for you. I was moved.'

'Do I get a consolation prize then?'

'I can't imagine any you could get – other than virtue's own reward.'

'You might love me a little.'

'On your own showing, a little is no good. Only the peaks are perfect.'

'We might try for one.'

'I think the law of gravity applies.'

'Which sort of gravity?'

'Both. I would want us to be grave, not cynical. *And* I think things have a tendency to go downhill. We'd have to start on the highest level.'

'Wasn't I there this evening?'

'Yes. You raised my standards.'

'So?'

'I'm afraid we mightn't come up to them. You're a lawyer, after all. You could probably have made as good a plea for the opposite school of thought: the gather-ye-rosebuds school. I suspect you of belonging to it.'

'I've been a temporary member. It's a matter of circumstance. One may change.'

'No, no. The passionate apprentice doesn't change, but waits.'

≈§ 90 §≈

'I'm older then you, *cara*, I couldn't have waited in celibacy until now. You're being a little hard.'

'I wish hardness were my trouble.'

In her bedroom, she put on her best nightdress and hoped he would not come. Later, she began to hope that he would. He didn't.

She finished reading the gambler's memoir, telling how he at last came home to Florence, married a girl with a dowry, had nine children by her and two by a slave girl from Tartary, then died in an odour of incense. Even then she couldn't sleep and had now nothing to read. Having put the light off, then on again, she got up and stood looking out at the moon-white olive grove. *Kyu*, called an owl, *kyu*. Tonight when he spoke of love and lust, had he meant her to wonder which he felt for her? Wasn't the distinction obsolete? Didn't one, nowadays, flow and change into the other? Yes, but *he* didn't belong to today and for him the vengeful old distinctions might be absolute. How absurd if they weren't, and she playing by old rules when he had adopted new ones! *Kyu*, went the owl's bleep. *Kyu*. The neat smug sound was like a summation.

Outside in the olive grove were live rustlings. She wanted to run out under its branches, smelling the night aromas. She wanted that sea of milky moonlight to lap, comfort and merge her with the lazy peace of the night.

It was two a.m. Putting on her slippers, she slid along the corridor, down the stairs and, after opening the outer door with some trouble, stepped out and then down some steps to the olive grove. Above and behind her, the villa was tightly shuttered. No light. Had she imagined that he too might be sleepless and, looking out, see her pale among the trees? Like a girl in a Tampax ad: afloat in a meadow of soft, ethereal grass, denying the inflamed matter within her!

Her coyness was as false as the ad and, in revolt against it, she had a longing to be fucked by some unpretending creature like a goat. Pan – maybe that was where the notion of him came from? From an urge for basic, bestial simplicity. What a lying, dim, servile, low, crawling state love was – or lust. That was probably what she was feeling. It *was* what she was feeling and if she'd been honest about it earlier she would be in Guido's arms this minute. Fool, she harangued herself. Liar! And crunched her way over harsh stubble. The grass had been scythed and was not soft and caressing at all.

Taking off her slippers, she ran along a stubbly aisle between olive trees for about a hundred yards, then back to collapse on ground which gave off a reek of wild fennel. Her feet were stinging with pain and her breath came in gulps, but she felt better. Turning on her back, she stared up through a web of olive leaves at the night sky. It was smudged with stars. Pale, sugary siftings of them: the Milky Way. The leaves on their thin branch tips shuddered, weaving and unweaving a hypnotic design of light and shadow. The sound of crickets rubbing their limbs together made an audible counterpoint to this and as she lay, dazed, exhilarated and, after all, caught up in the patterns of the night, she had a hallucinative sensation as though the starlight were somehow inside her body. She lay there for what felt like a long time.

When she finally rose and groped her way to the terrace, she was so tired and her feet hurt so badly that she scarcely noticed where she was going. When she tried to put on her slippers, she found that her feet had swollen and that a sliver of something had got under the skin of one heel. Limping, she walked along the terrace, in a door and up some stairs. Here the moonlight no longer reached and the corridor seemed curiously unfamiliar. Feeling about her for the light switch, she knocked down something which rolled about, then rebounded with a brassy clang. She stood for maybe a minute, waiting to see if someone would come to investigate, but nobody did. The light switch was not where it should have been and she began to fear that she had taken a wrong turning. There were two identical courtyards in the villa and if she had mistaken one for the other, she could now be heading in the wrong direction. Impossible to tell in the dark. Moving forward with greater care, she came to what seemed to be a familiar bend in the corridor with a door just beyond it which should, if she was on the right route, be the door to her own bedroom. Cautiously, she opened it, located the light switch in exactly the right spot and flicked it on. For a moment the dazzle blinded her. Then she saw a room which was not only not hers but seemed to belong to a different house. It was shabby and run down. the wallpaper was peeling. The only furniture consisted of a few packing cases, a small television set and a bed. Sitting upright in this was a bearded, naked young man. He was pointing a gun at her.

'Don't make a sound,' he told her in a low voice, 'and don't move.'

As he spoke, a side door opened and Neri slid into the room.

'*Calma*,' he said to the man with the gun. 'It's all right. You can put that away. It's Anne. I know her.'

The other man continued to point his gun at Anne. It had a silencer. She was almost sure that that was what it was.

'*I* don't know her,' said the man with the gun. His left arm was in a sling and she recognized him as the young man she had seen on her first evening in the window above the old stables. He was also, she thought, though she was less sure about this, the fugitive whose photograph had been in the papers. 'Who is she?' he asked Neri. 'A groupy of some sort? I'm fed up dealing with amateurs. I'm fed up being stuck here. I should have been away a week ago.'

'You'll be away soon. Put that thing down.'

'Why? Your security seems cockeyed to me. Bloody women strolling in at three a.m. I've a good mind to do her – and you.'

'Don't be a lunatic. They'd come looking for her.'

'They're probably going to come looking for *me* anyway. How do I know I can trust you?' The young man's gun hand trembled. 'Those pills you got me are making me sick. Why can't you get me to a safe doctor? I can't think how I fell into the hands of a kid like you. Bourgeois! Inept! *Figlio di Papa!* I want to get back to my own people or out of the country – not sit mouldering here. Who is this cunt?'

'She's OK. She's helping me. How do you think we get food and stuff?' Neri moved the man's gun-holding hand so that the gun was pointing at the floor. 'You're feverish. It's a side-effect of that stuff you've been taking for your infection. Go to sleep.'

Quickly, he drew Anne after him through the side door and shut it after them. 'What the hell are you doing here?' he asked in English.

She explained about getting lost. Neri looked suspicious.

This room too contained a bed and had the air of having been fixed up with bits and pieces from some attic. There were no rugs and the floor boards were unvarnished. A basin and ewer stood on a small table next to a portable bidet. Books, medicines and newspapers were piled on a packing case and a chair bore a stack of neatly folded clean linen. Neri pulled a heavy curtain across the door, put his finger to his lips, then: 'My father's here, isn't he? Spending the night?'

'Yes.'

'You'll have guessed who that is,' tilting his head towards the next room. 'I need hardly tell you that if he and my father were found under the same roof, my father's career would be finished. A police raid now . . .'

'There needn't be a raid. Your father could take his own measures ...'

'Listen,' Neri was leaning over her; his face was inches from hers. 'Don't meddle in what you don't understand. That man in there saw his comrades gunned down in cold blood by the police. So don't imagine he'd let himself be arrested quietly. He knows they don't want him alive. And he's *valuable*. He knows things.'

'How could you have brought him here?'

'It wasn't planned – look, this is no time for going into the hows and whys. He's here and I've got to get him away. So keep quiet. Don't say a word to *anyone* and he'll be gone in two days. I'm making arrangements. In everyone's interest. *He* is getting nervous. I can hardly control him. Well – you saw.'

Neri too was nervous. This was not the play-acting youth with whom she had chatted in the library. He was jumpy and on edge. He kept pausing to listen. 'OK then,' in a tense whisper, 'will you hold your tongue?'

'Jesus, Neri, how do I know you haven't got more people here? Maybe you have explosives and are planning some sort of coup? I'd be an accomplice and so would everyone in the villa. Maybe the safe thing is to call a halt ...'

'How do you call a halt to a live bomb? Hm? The thing to do is to get it away from people. That man's like a bomb. Give me a day. Two. There's been a hitch or he'd only have been here one night.

'You said you weren't in favour of violence?'

'I'm not. I'm not. But try separating two maddened dogs and see if you don't find yourself getting violent too. This man's a victim – but he's been maddened. Listen, have I your cooperation?'

'If you're trying to avoid a scandal, why not tie him up while he's asleep? Then hand him over.'

'To be killed? Christ, even my father wouldn't – I hope – want that.'

'Why not tell your father then? Trust him?'

'Look, Anne, my father is not a man of violence. I've said that and it's true. What he is is a man of the Establishment: good at not seeing what's under his nose. If he turned this man over to the police and then heard that he'd been found hanged in his cell, a routine event here, my father would *believe* that it was an accident. Or a suicide. Institutionalized violence is invisible to him.' Neri, his breath coming in short, impatient pants, was hissing from the strain of trying to convince Anne while keeping his voice down. 'He just can't bear to believe the status quo has to be overturned. It has such good points, you see: old wine, young girls ... Listen, my main point is that *he* is working on the case of the cabinet minister's son. OK? Now, if he rings up the police and says that his client's confederate – a key witness on the run from the police – has been here for the last ten days, do you think anyone will believe he didn't know? He'd be *ruined* – so spare him that, will you?'

'I'm sorry, Neri. This time you've got to tell me more. If this man is wanted by the law ...'

'The law! Do you know what "the law" means here? My father and liberals like him put all their energy into trying to get the laws respected – but the laws themselves ...'

'Oh, Neri, forget the tub-thumping. Just tell me about this particular man. Who he is. A witness, you say. OK. But why do the police want him out of the way – and why are you working against Guido's interests?'

'It's because I'm thinking about his interests that I'm trying to get this fellow out of here quietly.'

'Then what?'

'We'll get him to a safe place where he can talk to the press. *Then* we'll get the truth. The truth is the most subversive weapon you can use in a country like this. And in this case, our friend next door may be the only one who knows it – apart from those who want it hidden and are almost certainly very highly placed. My father, you see, is trying to prop up what he thinks of as "the democratic state", but he's so busy propping that he hasn't looked in years at what he's holding up. He's like a tired old caryatid holding up a temple which has turned into a brothel without her noticing. As to why the police want the witness out of the way, the answer has to be that he has information which has the government shitting in its pants.'

'But then you're *not* on Guido's side! Isn't he working for the government? Isn't his client a member of it?'

'You surely don't imagine that our government is a seamless unit? His client's colleagues are almost certainly framing him: standard procedure when an ally gets awkward. The government's coalition. Even the majority party is divided. Elements in it are in cahoots with the Right and the CIA. Others – including his client – want a deal with the Communists. Sh! Listen, you'd better go. I hear sounds next door. *He's* jumpy. He won't like your being here too long. *Will* you keep quiet?'

'Quiet with whom?'

'*Especially* with my father. Look, it's for his sake. He couldn't cope with something like this. He's a man whose brand of cleverness works *within a certain framework*. If you take him out of it he'll be helpless. You must stop thinking that because I'm twenty and he's forty-seven, he's wiser. In this situation I am. Truly. Trust me, Anne. I haven't time to tell you more.'

'You'll get that bastard out of here?'

'Yes.'

'OK then – for now.'

Neri kissed her. 'You'll be glad you agreed. You're not

just saving a life. We may expose – well, it'll become clear when he talks to the press. While you're waiting, get someone to tell you about recent scandals. They'll open your eyes. Sh. Don't upset our nervy guest.'

He opened the door to the corridor, told her how to get back to her room and lent her a flashlight to help her do so unobtrusively.

'Give it to Ida,' he told her. 'She'll get it back to me.'

'Does *she* know . . . ?

'Shsh! Ida knows as little as she can. She trusts me.' Neri smiled and for the first time that evening, Anne was reminded of how handsome he was: a freshly minted version of his father, burnished and brilliant like a new coin. Returning to her room she managed, at last, to sleep well and soundly.

Up early, she felt forlorn since Guido would now be gone. He must leave, he had explained, at the crack of dawn. Rome, politics, his case called him. How good of him, she thought, not to have talked of any of that last night. No shop. No swagger. Whereas Neri . . . The young man's agitated chatter showed his father up to good effect. She doubted if Guido was naïve, the way Neri said. It was far more likely that Neri was.

But was it not the poise she admired in Guido's approach to politics which disappointed her in his courting? How foolish to be disappointed and yearn for declarations! Vanity, she told herself, in the morning light, sheer vanity on her part. And now, she'd let this accomplished song bird slip from her hand and into the bush. He might not be back.

She went into the dining room. It was shuttered still, and snapping on the electricity brought back the night. His place at table was dishevelled by the trace of his gestures: a chair pulled back, a glass displaced, his damask napkin thrown as he had left it in baroque disarray. The sight brought on a sense of something lost, radiant and insufficiently enjoyed. It was like the theme from an *allegro* returning in a slow, elegiac movement.

Walking on into the small room where breakfast was served, she was astonished to find him there, looking ordinary, with his mouth full of brioche.

He had had, he explained, to put off leaving. Car trouble. Now he would have to borrow the Lancia and drive to Florence to pick up his other car. She could help him out if she came with him and then drove the Lancia back. 'Would that put you out too much? We can have lunch together. Then I'll have to press on to Rome.'

This reversal stunned her. Easily and ordinarily, they had brioche and coffee together, shaking out blue breakfast napkins and passing each other sugar and jam. Yes, she agreed, she would do that. No, no trouble at all. How soon did he want to leave? Ordinariness was a prop, a mask and a promise. The ordinary was durable. Like a *Good House-keeping* guarantee, it covered the hope inside her. Like the dull veil worn by Arab beauties, it was not for modesty only, surely, but also to ward off the forces in the universe which rage at human joy? Never say you're happy or the demons will rob you. Smear the beautiful child with ashes. Deep in your secret psyche, count your buried wealth.

'More coffee?'

'Thanks.'

He looked older in the morning light. The lines around each of his eyes were like the skeleton of a small fish. A lifetime's experience had left this small insignia, carved so lightly as to typify his Tuscan preference for the understated. Neri could be from anywhere. The engaging thing about Guido was his regional character: a man made in Florence, he fitted the landscapes which she also loved.

CHAPTER FIVE

It was still early when they got to Florence and Guido, having
calls to make, left her free to rummage through the palazzo
which had been shut up while his wife was at the sea. Even
at the best of times, it must be an inturned world. The dilapi-
dated outer wall concealed an interior which changed as the
sun rose from a dim, cavernous place to a grove of reflections.
Vines of sunlight reached over the roof to touch the petals
of a geranium in an attic window, slid down a patch of bright
stucco, caught the gleam of a fountain in the depths of a loggia
and in under an hour had webbed the area with crisscross
beams as complex as the warp and weft of a loom.

Shutters were being closed against the heat. The sound
of this happening echoed up and down the street. Until
evening, the world would remain divided: outside the relent-
less glare and indoors a slightly stuffy darkness smelling of
old furniture and privacy. Under a chest, wood dust, as fine
and bright as powdered cinnamon, testified to the destructive
activities of a worm.

'Anne!' Guido's voice reached her from somewhere in the
upper shadows.

'I'm down here.'

'Come and try these clothes.'

They had been Flavia's, he had explained on the drive in,
and she should see if they fitted her. The idea was faintly
repellent even though she had sometimes bought lace at

market stalls and made herself shirts from Victorian petti-coats. Those, after all, had been anonymous, and commerce had rid them of old wearers' ghosts. Perhaps he wanted her to rid these clothes of Flavia?

'They don't fit any of the women in our family and we haven't,' he had explained, 'been able to bring ourselves to throw them out. Flavia was terribly extravagant. It was part of her condition.'

He was waiting for her in a room at the top of the house.

'We call this the "English" room,' he told her and it did look English, being upholstered in sprigged pinks and greens with a skirted dressing table and two wardrobes in knotted fruit wood. These were open, showing ranks of suits and dresses of the sort which skilled dressmakers construct so that they hold their shape for decades. Jackets were archi-tecturally built, hand-finished and silk-lined. Hems were inter-lined, and snap-fastenings masked with camouflaging petals of matching silk. Sachets released puffs of desiccated scent.

'Is this a bit like raiding a tomb?' she wondered.

Guido pooh-poohed this. Some of the things here were back in fashion, he informed her knowledgeably. *La mode retro* was the fashion world's term for these cyclic returns of taste. 'Look,' he picked out a sheath of oyster-coloured tussore, let it ripple in the light, then held it against her. 'This goes back to her girlhood. Flavia would never throw anything away.'

She took it from him and was surprised to find it as light as straw. It moved like falling water. She craved it.

'It's too grand.'

'We'll lunch somewhere grand. Try it on. There's a dressing room in there. I'll wait.'

The dressing room contained a pier-glass, a tailor's dummy, a bowl of talc with a swansdown puff and a pair of wooden tongs for stretching kid gloves. These accoutrements of vanity were beguiling and reminded Anne of dressing up as a child in her mother's party clothes to play at weddings. There had always been a faint staleness to the cloth.

She slipped on the dress. It was more than a slipping on for there were concealed underpinnings and, though simple in outline, the crisp garment was meticulously built. Looking up from its complexities, she beheld in the slightly spotted mirror a girl of twenty-five years ago. All ease and innocence, the girl glowed within the silk's glow and Anne felt that the image in the glass was only provisionally her own. She was today's girl. Tomorrow someone else would stand in this sunlight, perhaps wear this dress. Things here had more substance than people. Feeling her mortality, she ran a finger along the outline of her breasts which the dress had lifted and improved.

They lunched in Fiesole on the terrace of an old convent which had been turned into a hotel. Drinking white Arbia wine in cold beaded glasses, they commanded a distant view of Florence whose terracotta roofs were bloomed by a mildew-blue haze. Guido said that she should visit the rooms of this hotel and for a moment she wondered what he had in mind, but it turned out that he had nothing in mind at all except that the place was interesting, having been furnished with antiques of the right period so that, unlike such houses as the Cavalcanti's, where things and people had worn out and been replaced haphazardly, this was all of a piece.

'A museum piece,' he said, 'perhaps too perfect!' And the thought intruded itself that the past's perfections might be a bit of a torment to the Cavalcanti.

She felt a touch too perfect herself in her luminous dress and the new, gilded sandals which Guido had insisted on buying.

'You can't wear your brogues with that dress!' he'd said

when Flavia's shoes had turned out not to fit. 'Let's buy you some sandals: a gift from my mother. We'll go to Ferragamo.'

She agreed but when they got to the shop he wanted her to try on court shoes as well and flats and dress sandals in various styles. Naturally, the saleswomen and manager were all over him, calling him Signor Marchese and pulling down box after box. The shoes, they exclaimed, looked magnificent on the Signorina. Anne agreed that they did but was firm about accepting only one pair of sandals. Made of a single gold thong and leather sole, these were cheap and it seemed silly to make a fuss when Guido insisted on paying for them.

'They're from my mother,' he insisted. 'You can thank her.'

However, as they left the shop, she saw a large box being carried out and stowed in the boot of his car.

'Money's a boring topic,' was all he would say when asked about this.

'Well, but I'd rather not have gifts forced on me.'

'Why not? Do you think they're snares? Bait? What do you think I want from you? I assure you I'm neither Mephistopheles nor a white slaver.'

'Sorry.'

'I should hope so.'

Now the shadow of a quarrel hung over them. With a younger man she would have had the thing out. With Guido, an impression was conveyed that all this was ground he'd been over before and didn't choose to revisit.

'Tell me,' she looked for a neutral topic, 'about Flavia.' She touched Flavia's dress.

'Poor Flavia! My mother miscalculated there. She thought that, if guided to the port of marriage, Flavia'd be all right. Unfortunately, marriage is not the haven it was.' Guido shrugged. 'How was a girl like that to accustom herself to stop gathering rosebuds – worse, how grasp that she was herself a gathered rosebud destined to wilt in a domestic pot-pourri?'

'So then?'

'The details are banal. Let's say she came to grief. By contrast, your mother . . .'

'Yes?'

He crumbled a *grissino*. 'She backed away from love. Played the coward. I've often wondered whether her marriage was happy.'

'Average, I suppose.'

'A pot-pourri?'

'Not that bad.'

'*Le pot au feu* then?'

'Tell me about Cosimo.'

'Cosimo was cover.'

'What?'

'A decoy. A fiction. I was your mother's lover.'

'You?' But she should have guessed. It was what everything pointed to.

'Yes. We were in love. I asked her during that Dublin interlude to come away with me.'

What was this arrest of her faculties? Jealousy? Of her own dead mother? I'm not hearing this, she thought. It's hallucinatory. 'To come . . . away?' she asked, testing them.

'Yes. She could have got a divorce in England. But she hadn't the nerve. I tried to insist and she went into recoil. Perhaps passion began to frighten her and your father's sheer tepidness spoke for him. I couldn't have foreseen *that* – that she would think me unreliable and choose *le pot au feu*. We were – I thought – in that state of volcanic eruption when anything seems possible. Why should we be held back by social considerations?'

So last night's speech had been an elegy. Anne felt a pain

and a paralysis in the roots of her tongue. It crept up her palate. It was as if Guido had driven some sort of metal pin or stake through her. Anne the vampire! The dress, the gold sandals and her hopes mocked her. So it had all been a misunderstanding?

He was talking on, giving details of letters he had written or not written. What he'd said. Her mother's hesitancy. His eyes, blind to her as two pebbles, saw nothing but the past. Then: 'You,' he said, 'naturally, I suppose, must side with your father.'

'Poor Daddy! Well,' said Anne, vengeful on behalf of both, 'perhaps she loved him best after all? She stayed with him.'

'In the end only. He was her second choice. I was her first. She promised to join me.'

'Ah,' Anne pounced, 'she made you leave?' It was a mean, small triumph but she wanted to jog his attention, get through his oblivion of herself. He was worse than oblivious. He was polite, showing her the menu, recommending artichokes and *veau poêlé* or, if she was hungry, a *bistecca alla fiorentina*, then returning to his old, crossed idyll.

'She appealed to my trust in her and swore ...'

Anne heard scraps and snatches. Naturally, her mother had let him down. Was *all* her pain for herself, she wondered.

'She turned you into a dream,' she told him. 'Something which need not be realized. Whereas my father ...' But, to be sure, Mummy had betrayed *him* too.

Procrastinating promises had been made for months to Guido whose go-between, a man at the Italian Institute, had then left Dublin. Later there had been someone at the embassy ... Two-faced, fence-sitting Mummy! In the end she had had to come clean, telling the embassy person that she and Anne's father were making a go of things and that, to seal their reconciliation, she had got pregnant.

'With you.' He looked at her at last.

'Me.'

'Yes.'

Anne began to laugh. It was funny in a horrible way. She had been conceived by Mummy to help patch up her marriage. Born to be a Band Aid! She wondered whether to share the joke with Guido but could see from his sober and baffled face that he was too absorbed in his own side of the thing.

'I hated you,' he was saying, while ignoring her inappropriate titters, 'you and your father.'

'Poor Daddy!' It was like a prayer this time. Help me, Daddy, fellow victim.

'Why "poor"?' Guido, a monster of selfishness, ate braised liver and chatted in an even voice. 'He won. I never fell in love again. Never. I married a cousin.' He shrugged. *'Le pot au feu.'*

And sired Neri and neglected him, she thought with a stab of sisterly feeling for this third victim. What Guido had left out of his chat on love was the havoc wreaked by lovers. Though he could no doubt justify that too with his lawyerly logic. Macchiavellian. Tuscan. How could she have admired it? Neri was right. Against such smugness only something direct and crude would serve.

'This is mostly fantasy, isn't it?' she said, trying for a bit of directness herself. 'Neither of you was all that much in love. You played at it for a bit. Now it amuses you to trot it out again for me.'

He looked startled. His own view, she saw, was gospel to him, and must have hardened over the years.

'Why should I lie?'

'Why should she? But she did. To me. Turned you into a fairy story, called you Cosimo and . . .'

'From shame. People who start to leap then don't are pig-in-the-middle for ever. The godlike Cosimo, appearing on his Dublin Horse Show horse then taking off like a creature in a fable, could be discussed as I couldn't. An avatar. That version absolved her.'

'Tell me what you used to do with my mother.'

Again that startled look.

'I want to imagine her happy,' Anne explained. 'Light-hearted. She never was. Not when I knew her.'

'But she had such a capacity for happiness! Everyone noticed it. You mean – she never recovered?'

Mollified? Pleased? She scrutinized him with malevolence. Did he feel no guilt? Did he even notice what he had done to *her*?

'Describe happy things you did,' she asked. 'One happy thing.'

'Oh, we used to go dancing in Florence. I don't think we were in love yet. It was an escapade. We went to funny after-noon dances held in artificial darkness. Lower-middle-class mothers used to bring their daughters there and sit watching while they danced. Some knitted. They sat on chairs arranged round the dance floor and watched. Their eyes were out on stalks. Naturally, our going was a secret from everyone at the villa. We were supposed to be playing tennis. Then we would dance cheek to cheek to scandalize the mammas. Eventually, we were thrown out and forbidden to return. A giggle, you know. A prank. We were able to feel daring at little cost. Nobody we knew went to those places. She was eighteen then. Was she really not happy when you were growing up?'

'Not really.'

Anne remembered a dispirited slattern flipflopping in slippers and not beautiful at all. Well, Daddy always thought she was, though Anne couldn't see it. Beauty required repose and Mummy was all moods. Some women's faces were said to be as 'pretty as a painting', but Mummy's had been more like a TV screen: an area of shadow and sudden change. Even in Anne's earliest memories her mother had an unsafe laugh and her husband, the bomb-expert, had handled her with care. Mild, patient Daddy! He was for ever taking defensive cover behind a book or in his carpentry shed. In the beginning he must have thought she'd liven him up then, when this went wrong, found himself using all his energy to keep her at bay. He never complained and was timidly pleased when she got herself up to accompany him to a party where, as he would later report with pride, she outshone the other wives. It was the one thing she could do for him and he was reassuring them both by noting that she was doing it still. Anne had been unable to work out why the two didn't want more out of life. At first she blamed her father but when he died saw she had been unfair. For years afterwards his undemanding face would flash up unsummoned in her mind. Why *should* he have been undemanding? Uselessly, she longed to demand things for him and it was in this connection that she first realized that she no longer believed either in eternity or prayer. Giving these up on her parents' behalf was more upsetting than her childhood fear of hell. It was appallingly finite. Account closed.

Doubly dead in memory, her father put a finger to his moustached lips. The moustache was like a gag, a muzzle, a device which made him sing small. Why should he have had to? Marmalade-coloured he had been. Domestic. Trained to come to heel. A good man. Too good for his own good.

Guido, a concerned look on his face, could have been a vigorous version of poor Daddy. He had the same colouring, the same high cheekbones and if he'd had a moustache – oh God! *Poor* Daddy! Was *that* why she'd married him?

'Did your affair with her start here? Before she went back and got married? Was it with *you* she had a love-nest in Florence?'

'Yes.'

Anne burst out weeping.

'Anne, please, what's the matter? I don't ... Oh, I suppose I've been selfish just now.'

'You have!' Sobbing, no longer sure for whom she was mourning in this tangle of treachery from which nobody seemed to have benefited.

'Don't hate me. Please. I want to make it up to you.'

'You can't. It's too late. It's *them* I want to make it up to. Mummy and ...'

'Anne, she's dead.'

'I know. I *know*.'

'Hush. Don't get your eyes red. You don't really know, you know. I mean about her being dead.'

'Them! *Them* being dead.'

'Them. Did you have religious funerals for them? With hymns and ceremonies? So as to say goodbye to them properly? In your mind?'

'I did. It didn't work. *Day of wrath, dread day of reckoning* was all too true. All I felt was rage.'

'With whom?'

'Myself for not being nicer to her. Her for making niceness difficult. I'm talking of *her* funeral. *His* was years ago, though that too ...'

'Listen, you've finished your veal. We can go and dance for a bit. It's more private. There's dancing in an arbour they keep for wedding parties. Try not to sniffle. The waiters will think I've done something awful to you. Have I?'

'Yes.' She was behaving now like a luxuriously spoiled child – but why shouldn't she? Emotion was brimming in her. It needed to come out and it was her turn, she felt with a vague but strong sense of self-justification. Hers.

'Come on.'

Threading their way past a trolley laden with puddings, Guido led her out, across a lawn and down some steps to a paved area where a few couples were rotating to piped dance music. Putting his arms around her, he backed her round the floor then into a leafy corner where he kissed her. Anne closed her eyes, then felt him dab them with a handkerchief.

'You've got tears all over me. Never mind. Let them be for her. Let's say goodbye to her together. Forgive yourself and her. You can't live in the past.'

'Isn't that what *you* wanted? Isn't it why you got me to wear this dress?'

'No. The past is gone, Anne. Dust hath closed Helen's eye.'

'Guido, are you using my mother to seduce me or me to revive my mother?'

'Anne, I'm not *using* you. You fulfil an old promise. I thought you'd understood that – that I didn't need to explain. I was just filling in a moment ago, letting you know about the past – the promise – so that we can go on from there. I've been trying to, oh, justify the fact that I'm painfully in love with you. You've been flirting a bit and putting me off a bit and I suppose that's because I seem like the classic philanderer in his late forties. You've probably been told that that's my reputation. And I suppose I have been that. But this is different. I know it and I don't know how to make *you* know it, so I've been invoking forerunners and – forgive me if I've been clumsy – trying to establish myself as a worthy figure. A pompous activity it seems now. I can see that. To a young girl it must seem that I'm trying to give myself a new virginity. God, every word makes it worse. May I be simple? Will you wipe the rest out and believe that I am more absolutely and terrifyingly in love with you than I had imagined possible?'

She said nothing.

'Anne?' His voice was hoarse. 'Please.' A pause. 'Say something.'

'I'm trying not to cry again.'

'Don't do that. We might be put out.'

'Like you and my mother.'

'Yes.'

'Then I won't. No repeats, Guido. No encores? All right?'

'A new thing?'

'Yes.'

At the last minute the marchesa sent word that she was not feeling up to joining Anne and the count for dinner and that they should entertain each other as best they could. The count was in an excitable mood.

'My eye!' He laid a finger to the side of his nose. 'Guido was in a prudent mood last night!' The finger moved to his lips. '*Acqua in bocca!* Mum's the word, eh? All that talk about love!' He tittered.

'I don't understand.'

'Exactly! He didn't want us to. Tsts! The country's in convulsions, the government tottering, Guido's in the thick of it and what does he talk about?' Bonaccorso nearly had a convulsion himself. 'Well,' he recovered enough to say, 'he must know some unedifying things about the un-Christian un-Democrats. Just as well to keep silent. Nowadays even your nearest and dearest can betray you.'

This seemed to set off a new train of thought; Bonaccorso's face grew gloomy.

'Did you see Cosa this evening?' he asked. 'How is she? She wouldn't see me. Never will when she's not well. Vanity. Not about her looks. About her stamina. Vanity survives but changes. Maybe it surprises a young thing like you to hear that it survives at all? Well, it does. A lot does. More than you'd think. Rage, jealousy. All the deadly sins. Perhaps not the virtues? No, I think not. *They* require innocence and energy. How is she?'

'I didn't see her either. I was in Florence and when I got

back she was having her injection. Ida says she's all right. Tired but in good spirits.'

'That's her!' said the count. 'That's young Cosa. I still think of her as young. I suppose that seems strange to you too? Well, I do. In my head she's the girl I knew fifty-five years ago. You, sitting there in your pretty dress – I should have complimented you on it – may think that absurd.'

'No,' said Anne.

'Well, neither do I. The couple is the smallest alliance: too small. There are terrible treacheries within it. If Cosa dies on me that will be one. She *could* hold on. Maybe that's why she won't see me? I might start to bully her about it. Have some port,' said the count. 'Let's drink to life.' He poured liberally. '*Zazdarovya*. To your health.' He raised his glass. 'And to death do you know what I say? I say *pogue mahone*.' He laughed. 'It will too. One of these days *et très bientôt même*, in the cold clay of that cemetery down the road, that's just what death will do. It'll kiss my arse and eat me arse first. *Pogue mahone*, death, *pogue mahone!*'

Unable to think of any rejoinder, Anne raised the glass he'd poured her and drank its sweet, heavy, blood-temperature fluid.

'A libation!' cried the count who had spilled some of his on the cloth.

Niccolosa held Anne's new sandals up to the light.

'From Ferragamo, are they?'

Standards of craftsmanship were not what they had been. She looked at them with an assessing eye. Propped by pillows, she was sitting up in bed and her hair formed a nimbus from which her face emerged with the dynamism of a prelate magnified by panoply. An officiating prelate. The gilded sandals took on a look of emblems. She seemed too intent on them. Possibly malign. With no change of tone she remarked: 'Guido's wife has been phoning. She wasn't able to get in touch with him all day yesterday and neither were his clients. At one point she grew so alarmed she feared he might have been kidnapped. Ida tells me that six pairs of shoes have been delivered for you.'

'Oh dear.'

'Yes?'

'Guido bought them. I left them at the palazzo.'

'Oh?'

'I didn't want them.'

'But *he* insisted?'

'It was,' said Anne, unsure whether or not she was lying, 'because of my mother.'

'So he told you about all that?'

'More or less.'

Niccolosa nodded. 'Men Guido's age,' she said, 'can be afflicted with regret. *Le démon du midi.* It's a folly, a sickness. The object of their regret is youth, but they tend to think it's something else. A woman usually. You must not believe anything he says when he's trying to make love to you. There are reasons which I'd rather not go into as to why you should keep away from him. You may imagine that it embarrasses me to have to appeal to you like this. I wouldn't do it if the reasons were *not* grave and, unfortunately, very private. I'm hoping I may count on you. May I?'

'To ... avoid him?'

Niccolosa stared lengthily at Ann. 'To be the sensible one. After all, this is a folly which afflicts his age, not yours. You may have been flattered by his attention, even touched, but I assume you are not deeply engaged and will be able to draw back without making him lose face. *Brutta figura* – loss of face – can make a man do all sorts of foolish things whereas, if seen to act well, he can be stoical, even heroic. Here are your sandals. As for the other six pairs of shoes – let's say they're a gift from me.'

Anne put on the sandals after some fumbling. Her fingers seemed to turn to water. Her face was so hot the skin felt ready to crack.

'Thank you,' she said awkwardly, then: 'Might it be better if I left?'

'Not at all. Why? You came to visit *me*. Do you want to cut short your holiday?'

'I'm not sure. I feel . . .'

'Embarrassed? But we can't have you leaving with bad memories of us. I should miss you, Anne, if you left now and *I* should suffer acutely from *brutta figura*. The fault has been all on our side. Don't rub our noses in it.' Niccolosa took Anne's hand. 'Think of Guido as of someone not answerable for himself. And don't let this poison your stay. Bad things happen between friends. If one gets over them the friendship is deepened. You will stay, won't you?'

'If you want me to.'

'Good. That's settled. Now perhaps I can ask you a favour? Maria-Cristina is coming here this afternoon. I couldn't put her off and I'm not up to seeing her. She upsets me. Will you see her for me?'

'Me? Why me?' Anne felt panicked. 'Couldn't Ida see her? Or the count?'

'Well, my dear, she knows you spent yesterday with Guido. I'm afraid someone let that slip. She kept telephoning, you see, and got rather hysterical. I would be grateful if you could calm her down.' Niccolosa's face was immobile. The wrinkles seemed to have been ironed out. Gingered and quickened, she sat, beaming her will towards Anne, bending her to say 'yes'.

'Yes, all right then.'

Anne groped her way to the door, then down the corridor to her room. There was a conviction about Niccolosa which persuaded her, on a level of herself with which there was no arguing or bargaining, that there was indeed some contaminating blight, some dread element in Guido's love. Back in her room, she pondered this. Might not the sickness be in Niccolosa herself? Was she not, by hypnotic sleight of hand, managing to project her own unhealth on to Anne and Guido so that not she but they seemed sick? Anne had heard of wise women in the Irish countryside using a healthy animal to draw the sickness from an ailing child which would then rise up cured while the animal went into a decline and died.

The conviction in Niccolosa's tone could have its source in just such a manoeuvre and so could the atmosphere in the villa. After all, the dying woman's distorted view of life must be affecting her entourage and Anne – because of Mummy's dying only six months ago – was vulnerable. I should go home, she thought. I shouldn't stick around. This house was like a conch sour with the smells and echoes of dead tides. If ever she and Guido were to get together it should be in a new and neutral place. Maybe I wouldn't care for him then, she thought. Maybe here in the villa he had become the focus of her own dischargings of sentiment and memory? A sort of lightning conductor? Probably, she should go home to Dublin and see. But leaving now so soon after Niccolosa's appeal would seem ungrateful and abrupt. Besides, Anne needed, for her own peace of mind, to know more about the web of secrets in which her emotions had got stuck. Feeling fouled by a guilt whose source was unclear, she was moved to do some moral spring cleaning, to open windows on dark places both here and in herself – but that, of course, was more easily thought about than done.

It was an hour to lunchtime. Time for a quick walk, she decided, and set off through the olive grove, taking deep breaths and long strides and beating the stubble with a stick to scare away vipers. Growing hot – the trees were planted too far apart to afford much shade – she made for the formal garden, a dank place designed around an inoperative sundial which no longer got the sun. The surrounding foliage had grown too high and the metal disc was green like an object dredged from a lake. Around it, however, grew a bed of wild strawberries where, burrowing under leaves, she came on some late, fat, sweet ones which she ate. She had a sense of her presence here as being intrusive but enlivening too, as the sun's would be if the foliage were to be clipped back.

Lunchtime. 'Well,' said the doctor, 'our lethargic police are suddenly as frisky as hunters in August. By the way,' he interrupted himself, 'I hope you're aware of *them*! I saw you in the olive grove. If you walk out like that you should wear bright colours and give the odd shout. Call out, "I'm a human being, not a rabbit!" Seriously, our sportsmen shoot whatever moves: butterflies, tourists, dogs. There's no game around here, you see.'

He had come to check the marchesa's health and been pressed to stay to lunch. *She* was having hers in her room.

'I suppose you've seen the papers?' he asked Anne. 'The terrorists are finally being picked up. Nets have been thrown wide and are being drawn in. Why now, one wonders, why not sooner?'

'Well why?'

The doctor's hands wove patterns of perplexity and cynicism. 'The terrorists' interests can coincide with the government's,' he said. 'When they do, they're given a long leash or even a nudge forward. They're infiltrated, you see. But they can get out of control. *Then* ...' He made a chopping gesture: edge of hand knifing inner arm. 'Pff! It's all blatant, but none so blind as those who will not see. Our politicians rely on our being blinkered by prejudice and, to be sure, we all *are* prejudiced. If we weren't, how could we function?

Supposing we had to make new assessments all the time? We couldn't. Our thoughts, *cara Signorina*, are ancient and recycled. Like coal, they're made up of old matter. They flame but they're old stuff. The voice of our tribe speaks through us.'

Guido's wife and cousin was a small, handsome-but-worn-looking woman dressed in tailored denim. Her skin was tanned to the colour of a cooked apricot and she spoke English with pretty inflections suitable for reciting a nursery rhyme.

'Well, Signorina,' she asked Anne, 'by whom are you now being fucked? By my husband or my son? Or both? It seems that your countrywomen are most robust.'

'By neither. What about you?' If there's one thing, thought Anne, that my countrywomen can do it's fight. A rush of energy churned through her: a sort of glee. She had been needing an outlet.

They were sitting in the drawing room by the drinks trolley. Dutch courage. Each had a glass beside her. A crack in the shutters had been opened and a blade of light cut the room in two.

'Oh dear,' sighed the little marchesa. 'I'd hoped you were going to be a great vamp and account for all their absences.' She eyed Anne who eyed her boldly back. 'Sorry about the rudeness,' said the marchesa. 'It was a shock tactic to make you spill the truth. Instead it's made you resistant, hasn't it? Try to see things from my side. I'm worried about them. There's a dark side to their lives just now and I'd be *relieved* to know they were making love not war.'

'If they are, it's not with me.'

'Lawyers and magistrates have sometimes been kidnapped and murdered,' said the marchesa instructively. 'So one worries about sudden absences.' A pause. 'Niccolosa persuaded you to see me?'

'Yes.'

The marchesa sighed. 'Mind if I smoke? Look, I know you spent yesterday with Guido. You were seen at Ferragamo's and later dancing in Fiesole. That's the sort of town Florence is. So, of course, I know there's something going on.'

'His car broke down,' said Anne, 'and ...'

'Oh, cars have a way of doing whatever Guido wants. The inanimate world is kind to him. The animate one too.' Smiling, drinking vodka, she looked at Anne without, it seemed, any anger. Why? Anne felt humiliated. Her fighting mood was leaking away.

'So you know everything. What can I tell you?'

The apricot face smiled on. It looked older than Guido's. This told against him who, instead, as Anne knew from Ida, was older than his wife. As on a badly erased blackboard, the marchesa's features showed half-cancelled expressions at the same moment as new ones. There was about her some of the incongruity of the broken doll left grinning in a corner of a child's toy cupboard. Nothing she could *say*, it struck Anne, could be more damning than that smile in the pretty, crushed face which the marchesa bore at a jaunty angle with chin up and an upward flick to mouth and eyebrows. *Bella figura? Brutta?* It was certainly under strain. Mummy and Guido, a pair of mismarried mate-batterers – emotional batterers, anyway, would have made an interesting match. As the old joke went: it had been a pity to spoil two houses with them.

I'm letting her put me off him, Anne realized. Does she know she's doing it? 'I don't know whether there's going to be anything between Guido and me,' she began, trying for accuracy, but, with a rush of resentment against the coppery, slightly demonic face in front of her and at the wilting of her own feeling for Guido, heard herself say: 'People seem to believe, though, that your marriage is a dead letter.'

The face didn't flinch. This made Anne feel worse. The woman must surely feel *something*. This was one of those sporting situations in which a rat and snake are put together in a ring. Neither may wish to fight but – it's hurt or be hurt. 'Why did you want to see me?' she asked.

'Niccolosa.'

'Oh!' The two smiled. Wry smiles. Snap. '*She* asked you to?'

'Yes.'

'And she's who told you about Ferragamo and Fiesole?'

'Yes.' A half-shrug. 'I think we are fellow denizens of her net. She is a spider, you know. Not perhaps a bad spider, perhaps even a kindly one. But she likes to be in control.' The 'Children's Hour' voice was disarming.

'Miss Muffet was frightened away.'

'But she likes to keep us close. Me anyway – but I think also you?'

'I can't think why.'

The atmosphere had changed. They were accomplices now, or at any rate there was a current of connivance between them. The marchesa let Anne refresh her drink and asked to be called Maria-Cristina. For a moment they circled away from the topic of Guido. She wanted to know about Neri. Here too, though feeling less reproached, Anne had to be reticent.

'It's a dangerous time,' said his mother, 'and I don't know where he is. New loyalties undermine old ones and perhaps he doesn't trust me. What he ought to know,' she looked meaningfully at Anne, 'is that he shouldn't trust the new people either. They may not be working for the interests he thinks.'

Anne remembered what the doctor had said at lunch. 'You mean they've been infiltrated?'

Maria-Cristina joined the fingers of one hand and shook

it. 'Some of those groups are *set up* by the police as traps. They create the groups so as to justify the emergency powers which they can then pressure the government to grant. A few genuine young people are sucked in ...' Another stare. 'He should know that.'

'I'm not sure I follow you.' Anne was not supposed to know about Neri. His mother too could be laying a trap.

'We live in a time of lies.' Maria-Cristina lit another cigarette. 'I said I came here because of Niccolosa, but that's only part of it. You see my family life too is a web of lies. Guido brings his professional habits home. He's a lawyer, an intriguer. He has no sense of what actually *is*. One could go mad. I don't know if you can imagine? It's like walking under water or through smoke so that you have to breathe all the time through special apparatus ... No, that doesn't quite describe it. Everything is filtered. You have to consider everything that's said and ask yourself: is this a lie and does it matter? I can go on for months being sophisticated – do you know that *sofisticato* means "adulterated with base materials"? Curious how a word can trip you up. Suddenly, I feel I need to know something for sure. I hoped to find something out from you.'

'But I'm an outsider here. What could I know?'

Maria-Cristina made a gesture signifying impatience and perhaps revolt. 'Guido,' she said, 'has had endless women. He used to give me a jewel for each major fling. Not for the quick ones. He'd have been beggared. My jewel box was a yardstick. Well, of course I took them.' She said this as though answering a question Anne hadn't put.

But Anne had gone into recoil: no matter how truthfully the other woman was displaying her feelings, her motive must be to work on Anne's.

'*Of course* I took them. Everything he gave me was so much saved for the family. It was so that I would do *that*

– anchor and restrain him – that Niccolosa got us married to each other. And I played my part until now. Now I'm tired of it. I don't really want Guido any more. At least I think I don't. One can become neurotically attached to the status quo. It's odd. When Niccolosa rang to warn me that he might seriously think of leaving me – oh yes, it was *she* who phoned *me*, my first reaction was a wild euphoria. A sort of glee. Isn't that odd? I'd been so afraid of that and then I realized I wanted it. The mood lasted some hours and then I began to think of, oh, houses, property, Neri's interests ... and something more obscure – habit? Memory? Something deep like a buried force with a powerful, irrational tug. That was last night after she rang. I didn't sleep. This morning she rang again.' Maria-Cristina's eyes wandered into some private perspective of memory. Then she shook herself. It was a self-nudge, a quiver like that of a cat preparing to do some necessary, feline thing. 'Years ago,' she said, 'I asked him for an annulment. He could easily have got us one. With his connections. It would have been legitimate too, for pressure was brought on us both ...'

'By Niccolosa?'

'By her and my parents. It would have been easy to prove. I was only eighteen when we married. I asked him to either get us an annulment or be a proper husband to me. I was twenty-five then.'

'He wouldn't?'

'No. He's like a child. Children hate to choose. I remember when Neri was small and I tried to teach him the meaning of the words "either or". I'd ask, "Will you have the apple or the orange, *la mela o l'arancia*?" He was three. He'd say "apple orange" and grab both. Guido is still doing that.'

'You're trying to put me off him, aren't you?'

'You haven't said whether you want him. I think I'm trying to see whether *I* do. Niccolosa told me that you were someone who knew what she wanted. *She* was trying to frighten me, but I thought: good, now someone will make a decision and I'll emerge from this maze of lies. But I get the feeling that you too are walking through smoke and that even if you do want him you don't know what this man you want is like.'

Maria-Cristina, who had had a third vodka, went on talking for a while.

'Well, you don't say much, do you?' she shot at Anne. 'Biding your time, is that it?'

But Anne got the impression that the other woman was wrestling above all with herself. Wrestling in the mud of memory and resentment as female mud-wrestlers – Anne had seen a two-minute sequence in the cinema – wrestled for money, delighting audiences by this ultimate violation of female taboos. Money was one of the constants in the marchesa's monologue.

'If you marry for property,' she said, 'you're very married. You wouldn't want to think all those years of wearing a social mask as stiff as ice had gone for nothing.' Her other theme was lies. Neri, while trying to break out of those which held his parents' world together, had perhaps fallen into a mesh of worse ones. 'I know he must have been here,' she said. 'He took my keys to this house.' Then she reached into her handbag and brought out a letter. 'Here,' she said. 'This may help you know more about Guido. It's a letter your mother wrote him years and years ago. I think he now thinks that their romance was very strong and pure but this shows that he let her down from the start. She was writing from Ireland or perhaps London. Anyway, she was hoping he would come after her, but he didn't. In the letter she remembers how he kept her hidden in Florence after Niccolosa found them kissing and made her pack her bags. She was upset because he wouldn't make love to her. She was a virgin, you see, and in those years if a man took a girl's maidenhead he had to marry her. A calculating chap was our Guido even in his prime. Here.' She handed Anne the letter, then rose to go. Her face was suddenly wizened like a fruit preserved in spirits and indeed she had downed a fair amount of alcohol. 'Don't worry about me,' she said. 'I drive well after a few drinks. I suppose this meeting may have been useful to us both. It may have cleared the air perhaps? Time will tell.'

After seeing her to her car, Anne strolled down the cypress walk. Her picture of things was a jigsaw into which new pieces must now be fitted: the image of Guido as husband. Not that she took the bitter wife's testimony for gospel. No, but a whiff of vodka and defeat lingering in Maria-Cristina's wake reminded Anne of Mummy in her truth-telling moods.

Turning back towards the villa, she found it transformed by the shadows of evening. These funnelled through the loggia, threw pilasters into deep relief and turned the classical harmony of daytime into a shape as stressful as that of a colony of shells or a fistful of matter held in a gigantic clench.

CHAPTER SIX

The letter from Mummy was date-marked Chelsea, London, October 1957. That was one year before her marriage and two before Guido's siege of it. Bad timing seemed to have wrecked this love affair. Mummy, having lurked wistfully for three months in Florence, was hoping Guido would defy his mother and join her in London where she was hiding from her own parents. Obsessively, the letter retraced the smallest moments in her short time with Guido. It covered eight pages, was written in loopy, extravagant handwriting and brimmed with endearments which Anne preferred to skip.

Do you know [ran the first unembarrassing paragraph] what most depressed me during those weeks while your mother thought I was back with my parents and *they* thought I was with her at the sea? It wasn't the lying and knowing I'd be found out. Nor even the fact that you wouldn't make love to me properly – oh, why wasn't I able to say things like *that* to you until now? The question frightens me. Does it mean I've nothing now to lose? Perhaps I won't post this. I should be fun and alluring – but wouldn't it shame us both if I were to crumple this letter up and start a witty, mistressy one to win you over? Or would it just be wise? I *shan't* be.

What depressed me most was a napkin ring. I'm not being whimsical.

I was a nomad, you see, in Florence, in August, with nobody

there but tourists and mistresses and me who wasn't quite either. Everything about the place suggested the bivouac: the tourists' coaches, those market stalls which are dismantled every evening and trundled off with the stuff sold from them during the day: leather goods, bolts of cloth, views painted on satin, plastic sponges, ash trays with pious or obscene messages, even the salesmen who are themselves for sale and turn up in the more modest eating places with a different foreign woman every three days. You'd think they'd get the women to take them to better places – but maybe they like to show them off. I ate in one called Il Fagiano on evenings when you had to be with your mother – you'll remember that there were more of those than we'd expected. So I became a regular and used to bow to the three other regulars: an accountant, a teacher and an English girl who was the mistress of the Marchese Cini and had been hoping for five years that he'd leave his wife for her.

'Well, we'd have to emigrate,' she told me. 'There's no divorce here, of course, but he could get a Mexican one.'

We had coffee together a few times and she told me she lived from giving English lessons. Her skin wasn't what it must have been and her hair was lank. Every evening she and the accountant and the teacher bowed to each other and each had their own table and a napkin ring of a distinctive colour supplied by the restaurant who could thus give them the same napkin for a week and save laundry. Hers was blue. I asked her if the Marchese Cini ever came to the Fagiano. I was worried because I'd met him at the villa and was afraid that if he saw me he might mention this to your mother. But it seemed that he never did come because they only met in out-of-the-way places where he wouldn't be recognized. She said she'd become a crack shot with rifle-range rifles, and talked of the outdoor cinema screens on the Lungarno with the furry haloes of mosquitoes which collect around them and the way the breeze can distort the images. She was funny and bracing about all this and I could see she'd learned not to be down in the mouth for she kept saying things like: 'I've a carriage horse's view of this city. I never get *inside* houses, you see. I'm usually not even inside the city. We meet mostly at rallies and firework shows and carnivals.

I'm expecting to be asked one of these days if I've a licence to attend. I'm such a fixture. The smell of nougat and barley water and hot pizza means Florence to me.' She said she was glad nobody at the Fagiano knew about her and the Marchese Cini. She was 'la Signorina' there and had their respect and her blue napkin ring. I could imagine her still there ten years later. It horrified me. Really. When in my third week of coming there I found a napkin ring at my own place, I decided not to go back.

Anne put away the coy, beguiling letter. It embarrassed her. She could see why Mummy hadn't gone away with Guido when he came looking for her two years later.

It had rained during the night. A skin of wrinkled damp clung to windowpanes, and spillages from gutters were apt to drench people crossing the courtyards. After breakfast, the sun came out and was refracted by prisms of water hanging from torn hibiscus blossoms.

Niccolosa was playing Monopoly against herself. Anne, paging through an album found in the library, came on a snapshot showing Guido and her mother in a festive group of young people. *Pienza*, said the caption, *June 1956*, but the celebrated architecture had been undermined by a tilting camera. It must have been a winey afternoon. Girls laughed. Wind snapped at scarves. A youth waggled his ears. The faces of her mother and Guido were small and inexpressive.

Niccolosa lined up wooden houses on the Monopoly board and smiled. She had shown no interest in hearing about Anne's talk with Maria-Cristina but was anxious to keep her occupied. Running through a list of suitable interests for her guest, she came up with antique-collecting. Did Anne know anything about Tuscan furniture? No? Well, she could combine business and pleasure. Niccolosa needed a lectern for the library. Her hands had grown too weak to lift the dictionary and she needed a large wooden lectern of the sort that came from churches. She knew just where Anne might find one. An instructive outing.

'You'll enjoy it,' she promised. 'Signor Pei has a splendid warehouse. Country priests sell him things for a song. He goes out with his lorry and brings back marvellous pickings. Tell him to give you photographs of anything he thinks I might like. But use your judgement too. Examine the state of the wood. Worm holes,' she advised, 'should not be parallel to the surface. That means the object was made recently with old wood.'

So Anne drove once more into Florence and, since Guido was in Rome, out of temptation's way, went straight to Signor Pei's back alley. His shop front was small and he himself looked like a gnome fresh-hatched from one of Hieronymus Bosch's eggs. He was sitting on a high stool reading something when she arrived and his chin almost touched his knees. The dome of his forehead gleamed at her. A moment later so did his eye. He had a quick, crooked, clever, friendly grin.

How was the marchesa, he asked. And her library? That, he said wistfully, was a treasure trove. He knew foreign buyers who would pay handsomely for items in it. '*Profumatamente!*' He rubbed thumb and index finger. Some were national treasures, their export forbidden, but the foreign buyers would pay the needed bribe as well. He laughed with enjoyment, revealing a mouthful of astonishingly individualized teeth. 'Americans,' he said, 'Germans. They all do it. *Tutto il mondo è paese.*' Tickled by the universality of corruption, he uncoiled his body, descended from his stool and led her through a series of vaulted cellars. 'They close an eye.' That was how to get business done, he explained, and guided her past a bristle of broken furniture. Bribes speeded things up. Why not? Florence had been a merchant city from the start. Built on business. Merchants put up with the brutishness of invading princes when they had to. Later, they'd fleece them by lending money at usurious rates. 'Fox and crane,' said Signor Pei. 'Each to his method. You learn to deal with everyone – well almost. Our latest scourge is the Communists. Letter-of-the-law men. Since *they've* started getting elected to municipal office it's hard to do business. They don't understand bribery.' He made a comical face. 'They're crippling the economy. Frightened of their shadows. Frightening their coalition partners. On every committee there's a Christian Democrat, a Socialist and a Communist. When I want a permit to export I have to have a stamp on it from each of the three and by the time I get it my client has either lost interest or died. Tell the marchesa times are terrible for the trade. Stock is low. She wants a lectern?' He was leading Anne through a forest of mutilated cabinets.

'This is unrestored,' he explained. 'I don't restore until I have a customer. You can go to fancy showrooms along the Arno and see things polished and presented with style. Do you know where they get them? From me. And they'll charge you three times what I do. There's a wedding chest. Umbrian. Sixteenth century. Needs a bit of work but it'll come up lovely. Mind your head. The ceiling dips here. I'm taking you to see a lectern. Not a great piece. Tell the marchesa the priests are afraid to sell. It's illegal for them to alienate property. Belongs to the State, you see. Never mattered when we had Catholics in the town hall, but the CP are great guardians of the national patrimony. Here's the lectern. Made of cheap wood. *Gattice.* That's poplar in English. Excuse me, there's the telephone.'

Dodging like a woodland animal between groves of candelabra and a kneading trough filled with broken angels, he picked the receiver from a telephone incongruously located among these oddments.

'Yes,' he said, 'she's here.' He beckoned Anne. 'For you.' Discreetly he moved off into a labyrinth of gilded pilasters.

Anne took the phone. It was Ida. She sounded aghast. There was a crisis, she said in a muffled voice. Il Signorino Neri had asked her to get hold of Anne. The person Anne knew about had got suddenly very ill. He needed to be driven to where he could be looked after in safety. Neri, unfortunately, was in Rome and the aforesaid individual – Ida, in her agitation, spoke like a bureaucratic form – was in urgent need of care. 'Drive round the back,' she instructed, 'and park as close to my door as you can. All right?'

'All right.' Anne put back the receiver. It seemed to be her role to be put in situations where there was no saying 'no'.

As soon as she reached the courtyard Ida emerged from her door. One outstretched arm held aloft a six-foot-high folding wardrobe made of vinyl. It did not quite clear the ground. At a nod from Ida, Anne opened the back door of the car and the flexible wardrobe was bestowed in a seated posture on the back seat. Ida sat next to it, holding the top part upright.

'Turn quickly,' she told Anne, 'and drive through the village. I'll get out just beyond it. That way it will look as if you'd given me a lift. Then take the road for Arezzo. You're to meet someone there in the station car park and hand over your passenger.' She indicated the wardrobe. 'Call him Franco. He's had a bad reaction to some penicillin we gave him for his infected wound and needs to get to a clinic. A *special* clinic. I've written out your directions for when you reach Arezzo. Here.' She handed Anne an envelope. 'Il Signorino Neri is driving up from Rome but that will take him a while. A third party is to take Franco from you in Arezzo and meet up with Neri. You just turn round once you've handed him over and come back as fast as you can. You'll be late getting back so I'll have to think up some story to tell the marchesa. Stop in at my flat before you see her. This is a corporal work of mercy,' she added, falling into what sounded like a memory of childhood catechism lessons. 'It's hard to know what to do for the best, Signorina Anna, but we could hardly let the poor young man die, could we? Here, slow up. This is a quiet stretch of road. Do you see anyone? No? Well, here goes.'

Ida unzipped the wardrobe and slid out of the car. She banged the door and waved Anne on. Turning to look behind her, Anne saw the bearded man who had pulled a gun on her two nights before. He was limply lolling and still partly surrounded by the shell of the collapsed vinyl cover which now looked curiously like one of the dark dominoes worn in Venetian carnival paintings. His head had fallen sideways and his face was sweating. The tinted car windows threw green reflections on to his cheeks, making him look sicker than she hoped he was.

Forty minutes later, Anne drew up in the Arezzo station car park. She opened the envelope and found a note telling her to go to a bar visible from where she sat and order a *caffè corretto* with grappa and a packet of *biscotti di Prato*. Her passenger hadn't said a word during the drive and was still slumped in his vinyl cover in a corner. From time to time he seemed to shiver although his face was still pouring with sweat. His breathing was irregular and occasionally he gave a small, sudden snore.

'I'll be back,' she told him. 'I'm going to that bar over there. OK?'

He gave a sort of grunt. She locked the car door and crossed to the bar, a small one decorated with the usual ads for Cynar, Negroni and Pilsen Beer. A blind man was selling lottery tickets at the door. Anne went in, asked for the ladies' room, used it and, coming back to the counter, ordered a *caffè corretto* and a packet of *biscotti di Prato*. Staring over the barman's shoulder into a large mirror, she examined the rest of the premises. She was hungry and thought of ordering a toasted sandwich but reflected that this might spoil the signal. Maybe she shouldn't have gone to the loo either? Her hand shook as she raised the cup to her lips. She drank the coffee slowly. The bar was empty except for two German tourists eating pizza at a small table. The lottery-ticket vendor had moved away. She made her coffee last as long as seemed normal, paid and wondered what to do next. 'Franco' was in no state to advise her. Perhaps she should phone Ida? She turned to leave.

'Signorina?'

The barman was busy cleaning the chrome counter.

'Did you call me?'

'Signorina Anna?'

'Yes.'

'Here.' He handed her a box of *biscotti di Prato*. 'You were forgetting these.'

'Thanks.'

Back in the car, she opened the box of biscuits and found a sheet of paper inside. There was writing on it. 'Arezzo contact no good,' it said. 'Meet me in Orvieto Cathedral. Try every half-hour from four p.m. Neri.'

'Shit!' The *biscotti di Prato* tasted sweet and stale.

No sound from the back seat.

'Are you all right, Franco? Hey, wake up. Do you want to go to the lavatory?'

'Piss – by side of road.' Franco's speech was slurred.

Of course, she remembered. His photograph had been in the papers.

'Can I get you anything from a chemist's while we're here? Do you want a drink?'

The answer was incomprehensible. Franco seemed to have passed out.

Finding him a place to relieve himself wasn't easy. It meant leaving the main road and even then there was not much cover. No hedgerows. The land was cultivated right to the road's edge. Peach orchards and olive groves were sparsely planted and vines hung thinly on trees instead of being set in camouflaging rows. Wheat and grass had been cut to the stubble. In the end she drew up next to a clump of tall reeds, half pulled her passenger from the car and pushed him in their direction. He had engulfed himself in the clump before it struck her that it might be growing in a marsh. He did, however, emerge. She supported him back to his seat and was about to get into her own when a car drew up behind her and a man got out and walked towards her.

'Signorina.'

Her heart began to hammer. The man was holding a small open booklet in his hand. It looked like an identity card. Police? she wondered. But agitation had blurred her vision. The thing in the man's hand was a blob.

'Virgin?' asked the man in English.

She stared.

'Pregnant?' he added questioningly. 'Where?' He held the blob under her nose. By now she could hardly see him, much less what he was holding. Could I, she wondered, be about to faint? She never had fainted in her life but this felt danger-ously like the preliminary phase: dizzy, weak and seeing black. Pull yourself together, Anne! She drove her nails into her arm and her vision cleared. So, to some extent, did her head.

If not the police, could this be a confederate of Neri's talking perhaps in code? His English had a foreign ring – meaning not Italian. German perhaps? But since the terrorists – and therefore the police too – were known to have international affiliations, this neither explained nor eliminated anything. She managed to cast a quick, casual glance – she hoped it *looked* casual – in Franco's direction and saw that his head was bent over and his face hidden.

'Talk Italian,' she directed. *'Lo dica in italiano.'*

'Madonna!' The man prayed or maybe swore. He handed her his booklet. It showed a very pregnant lady in a blue dress. Her hand, creeping across blue, pleated folds, revealed a slice of white undergarment gently curving down the melon-sized belly. The effect was tranquil and sensuous. 'Piero della Francesca,' read the caption, *'La Madonna del Parto.'* So this was – was he? – merely an art-lover, a lost tourist looking for help! Anne's own belly heaved. 'Near here,' insisted the maddening though harmless pest. 'Grotto . . . You direct me?'

'I don't know. I don't know.'

Her stomach, overcome by alternations of fear and relief, rose and she rushed into the clump of reeds where she brought up her *caffè corretto* and her *biscotti di Prato.*

Inside the cathedral at Orvieto, the usual few elderly women sat emptying their tired minds and a group of Americans appreciated the art of Luca Signorelli whose fresco depicted, as their guide was informing more people than perhaps wanted to hear, the fall of Antichrist, the sun, the moon, the Destruction of the World, the Resurrection of the Body and the Descent of the Wicked into Hell.

Anne circled the dusky interior, in search of a lurking Neri. Pillars were wasp-striped in – the flat-vowelled guide supplied this fact – limestone and basalt. Windowpanes were of alabaster and the effect was of holding a series of seashells to the light. The golden filterings, the writhings on frescoed walls and the materials used in the architecture gave the great enclosure the look of a natural phenomenon like a drowned cave. Having walked up one aisle and down the other, she was about to cross the transept when a voice hissed:

'Anne.'

She could see no one.

'Here to the right,' cried the guide, 'also by Signorelli, we have the Death of the Two Witnesses, a work of bold conception worthy of comparison with . . .'

'Anne.'

'. . . Michelangelo at his . . .'

'Sister Anne, Sister Anne!'

The Bluebeard hiss was coming from a confessional just near her. She slid into the penitent's section, knelt on the kneeler and put her eye to the dark grating.

'Is there anyone coming?' asked the manic shadow behind it. 'How's our invalid?'

'Damn your eyes, Neri. Do none of you ever grow up? I suppose you had an English nanny too? What did those women do to you all?'

'Fee fi fo fum, I smell the blood of an Irish womb! The nannies were our Sandhurst. How is he?'

'Neri, he's sick. *I* can't tell how sick. You'd better bring your car to where I'm parked right now so we can do a quick transfer.'

'Anne, I haven't got a car. I got here in a taxi. I've no transport. I need the Lancia.'

'And what about me?'

'You'll have to come with me. We'll get him to a pick-up point not, I hope, too far from here. Then I'll drive you back to the villa.'

'I don't trust you, Neri. How do I know you'll get me back? I hate all this.'

'My dear, I didn't choose it. It chose me. Destiny . . .'

'Balls, Neri. If you're working for any sort of a sane organization, how come they left you so badly equipped? How do I know they exist? Maybe you're mad.'

'Franco exists.'

'Let's go back to him,' she said in a rush of nervousness.

This, like an egg-and-spoon race in which the egg was a live bomb, was clearly an operation safer to finish than to interrupt.

'Why,' she asked as they walked back to the car, 'come here in a taxi?'

'My car broke down in Chiusi. No hired car available. I was lucky to find a local man willing to run me up here.'

'There seem to be a lot of breakdowns in your plans. Who are you working for? I think I've a right to know.'

'A group. One doesn't know more than one has to. I can't tell you much.'

'Do you *belong* to this group? Where did you meet them?'

'At the University last year. I was in law school. I belonged to another, affiliated group which was dissolved. Someone contacted me for this job. Originally, it was just to act as driver from one point to another. Bringing Franco to the villa was a last-minute emergency solution. Something went wrong with the place where we were planning to bring him so we had to use initiative.'

'We?'

'I wasn't alone then.'

'Why are you now?'

'The police have been catching up with a lot of comrades. They're unusually active. It just shows how important Franco is.'

Was there a skip to his walk? A swagger? She would have liked to beat sense into him. A nannyish urge, she reflected, and held this against him too. By now, however, they were at the car. 'Franco' acknowledged Neri without enthusiasm, but his complaints lacked vigour. He was too ill to say much. Where were they heading, he asked. Neri said he had to make a contact before he would know this. He took the wheel.

'You must understand,' he told Anne, speaking in English for greater security, although Franco's head had sunk on his chest and his heavy breathing showed that he had relapsed into some sort of stupor, 'that our group, the group I belonged to, were not conspirators. We wouldn't have helped Franco's people if *they* were conspiring either. We believe that when it comes to conspiracy and terrorism the people are never the users, always the used. It doesn't look that way, of course, so what we're trying to do is show up the *government's* conspiracy. Blow the whistle on it. They don't often give us a chance. This time they've handed us one on a plate.'

'Why should a government conspire? They're in power.'

'Their power is precarious. Capitalism in Italy is collapsing. So what can a government do? It can create a fake conspiracy against itself so as to unify the country behind it. Unfortunately, they have to *keep* doing this. Every time there's a public outrage they gain support and unity. Then the unity unravels; the support peters out. They have to start over. This time they've implicated a member of their own cabinet who was known to be planning an alliance with the CP.'

'Guido's client?'

'Yes. They couldn't fight him at the urns because he's popular, but showing his son to be a terrorist will destroy him. It will also scuttle plans for bringing the CP to power for a while – and unify the electorate.'

'*Was* the son a terrorist?'

Neri shrugged. 'Who knows? Who cares? If they can smear him and his father through him, that's all they need.'

'And Guido?'

'He's an innocent. He tries to fight by legal means.' They had reached the outskirts of the town. Neri drove into a garage. 'This is where I make my contact,' he told Anne. 'Have them fill up with petrol. Then park by the roadside and wait for me. I won't be long.'

She did this. Franco's rough breathing sounded to her like the beat of some sinister timepiece and Neri's absence began to seem interminable. Various sorts of discomfort assailed her. She needed to get out and use the lavatory, but hesitated to do so. Images of Neri fleeing back to the car pursued by God knew what danger checked her. She was hungry too. The last dry *biscotto di Prato* took the edge off this need but set up a new one when a crumb stuck in her throat and started a coughing fit. As this, aggravated by fear of attracting attention, grew worse, she decided, after all, to go to the garage lavatory for a drink. Blindly, eyes watering, she stumbled out and, on her way back, passing the window of the garage office, caught a glimpse of Neri sitting with his back to her. A young man in overalls was intently talking and nodding as though trying to impress some warning on him. Neri must have tried to interrupt for the young man raised his hand in the peremptory signal that stops traffic. '*Si,*' he was saying. She could lip-read the word through the window. '*Si! Si!*'

Back in the car, she sat listening to the churring of crickets and Franco's breathing. He sounded very sick. Then Neri returned. He looked glum and was sucking the insides of his cheeks.

'Shit!' He fumbled ineffectively with his seat belt.

'Let's go.' He took the wheel. 'Are you hungry?'

'Yes. But I can wait till we've got him to help.' She was worried about Franco. Supposing he died on their hands?

'I'm in a quandary about that. I've had bad news.' Again they were talking English. Franco, in the back seat, released a queer, dry, rattling sound. Neri's face was a knot of concentration as though he were mesmerized by the unwinding road. For a kilometre or so he said nothing; then he stopped the car. They were, as far as Anne could see, in the middle of nowhere. There was no landmark or likely indication that this might be the site of a rendezvous.

'Franco.' Neri leaned into the back of the car and shook Franco's shoulder. 'Are you all right? Need anything?'

Franco did not open his eyes. His head rolled and lolled.

Neri produced a small packet. 'Sandwiches,' he said. 'There was a vending-machine in the garage. Let's sit by the side of the road. I need air.' They got out and he closed the door behind them. 'Here.' He handed Anne a sandwich wrapped in cling wrap. While she was struggling to open it, she heard him say, 'I've reason to believe that Franco is a policeman. A stool pigeon.'

She looked up, ready to laugh: another Neri joke, but saw at once that it wasn't. Neri suddenly looked very young. He bit fiercely into the sandwich, stuffing his mouth as though to gag or steady himself.

In the car the invalid was still slumped over and the windows were rolled up.

'Well,' she said after a while, 'what shall we do then? Dump him?'

'It seems,' said Neri tonelessly, 'that *he* may have been dumped on *me*. The plan could have been that he deliberately get himself caught at the villa so as to discredit my father. This would explain his escape from the police shoot-out. I should have wondered about that. Odd that he should escape when the other two were so efficiently gunned down.'

'But he was wounded.'

'A mistake – and one which may have saved us. He couldn't get to a phone right away because there aren't any in that part of the villa. Then his wound got infected and he got even sicker when I got him penicillin. Probably he'd have been meant to contact his colleagues to let them know where he was. They couldn't know I'd take him there, though they no doubt hoped,' said Neri sourly, 'that I would. There or to our palazzo in Florence which would have suited them just as well.'

'So you think someone in your group . . . ?'

'Set me up? Maybe. Or was used to set me up.'

'Was the car that broke down supplied by them?'

'Yes. The other hitches could be explained by this theory too. The longer he was left on my hands the more likely it became that I'd be caught with a supposed terrorist. The fact that they didn't raid the villa can be put down to the notorious inefficiency of our police. There are so many parallel services, as they're called, each working in secret from the other, that they fuck up all the time.'

'Another explanation is that this new bit of information is false.'

'Don't think I haven't been worrying about that.'

'So?'

'I think the best thing to do is to deliver him as planned to the underground clinic run by his group. I'll pass on the rumour and let *them* deal with him.'

'Kill him?'

'That's not my affair.'

'But Neri, that would be murder. A lynching. You *can't* let them do that.'

'Well, if I hand him over to the police and he's *not* one of them, *they'll* kill him. No matter who he is, he knows too much about the Rome shoot-out – and about *us*. If he's a cop he's a shit and deserves what's coming to him.'

'Jesus Christ, Neri, I can't believe what I'm hearing.'

'They're the class enemy.'

'Who are?'

'Cops.'

'What class? Whose class?' Anne had the feeling of having got involved with a child or a lunatic. But the thought wilted as fast as it came. After all, the set-up here favoured lunatics and children. Maybe, where reality was so slippery, only they could survive? Humane, moderate behaviour required trust and an expectation that it would be reciprocated. Maybe *that* was what Guido was trying for? Wasn't his effort to work by legal means an act of faith in trust – and how else did trust ever get started? Whatever about that, Neri's readiness to abet lynch-law was brutish. It was also familiar. Anne had been to college in a Dublin where there was a strong current of sympathy for the tactics of the IRA. Perhaps if her own father had not fallen victim to these she might have felt that way herself? There is a persuasive appeal to the notion of cutting the Gordian knot – until the knot turns out to be made from a mesh of human limbs.

'The police,' Neri was saying, 'are the enemies of the proletariat which . . .'

'To which you, *Signorino* Neri, do not belong – and to which *they* do. Who the hell do you think policemen are? They're working-class boys who join the police because they need money, just as my father joined the army because *he* needed it. They may be brutal. They may be used against their own class, but the manipulators, the ones who *use* them, come from your class, Neri, yours and your father's. If it comes to that, I don't think *you* give a damn about people or politics at all. I think your manoeuvres are all aimed at Guido. You want to score off him.'

'I was trying to *help* him.' This came out as a sort of scream. 'To get evidence for his case.'

Silently, they munched their way through the remaining sandwiches. Then:

'What are we going to do?'

Neri shrugged.

There was a smog of hostility between them.

Anne stared at the slumped hulk in the back of the car. 'He's harmless now,' she pointed out. 'Why not give him a choice? Ask him if he wants to go to the underground clinic or to a regular hospital. Tell him his cover's been blown. He's got to get *some* medical care soon.'

Neri's smile was sour: 'A perfect dilemma for a man of

his sort. He's got to declare himself for or against the police.'

'Ask him.'

'OK. I will.' Neri walked over to the car, stared for some moments through the tinted glass windows at the man inside, then opened the door.

'Franco!' Neri shook the heavy, sweating, fevered body, 'Franco. Wake up! Listen! Can you understand me?'

It took a while before he got a response. Anne turned to tidy up the scraps of cling wrap. She could hear Franco grunt and Neri ask the same question over and over. Franco uttered a curse, groaned, then clammed up. Neri kept trying to rouse him.

'Shall we go to the police?' he asked, trying shock tactics. 'The police!' he whispered sharply and began reciting the initials of the various secret services. 'The DIGOS,' he whispered seductively. 'Do you belong to the DIGOS? Do you? Or the SISDE? The SISMI? The CESIS? Or some secret, secret one we've never heard of? Franco? Say.'

'Maria,' groaned the sick man, 'Maria, help me. I'm sick. I'm very sick.'

'Or the secret clinic? Would you rather go there?'

'Maria, please,' muttered Franco. 'Please, *please*.'

'Do you want to go to the Pronto Soccorso?'

'Be patient with me,' begged Franco, *'Mariuccia mia!'*

Neri came back to the side of the road and sat down. 'It's no good. He's beyond making sense.'

Anne walked to the car. 'Are you a stool pigeon?' she asked Franco and took his face in her hands. 'Are you a policeman?'

For a while there was no reply. Then Franco opened his eyes. 'I'll need fresh underwear,' he told her and closed them again. 'Can you pack some, Mariuccia?'

Anne and Neri stared at each other. Neri took a deep breath.

'Well, we'll follow our own interest. The secret clinic isn't far now. We'll take him there.'

But it was another hour's drive through wriggling, hilly land past small farms, chestnut woods and shaved fields before Neri drew up in the dark beside a small church flanked by a few wind-bent cypresses. With Neri's help, Franco managed to stumble out of the car. The vinyl wardrobe stayed behind. Anne didn't see the faces of the people to whom he was handed over. Neri spoke to them rapidly, conveying his warning. There were no goodbyes.

More driving, the headlights picking up curves which rushed frighteningly forward as the car lurched around them.

'*Piano*, Neri!'

'It's not true that I wanted to score off my father. Not true at all.'

'All right.'

Dark, woodsy scratchings at the windows of the car. He had run off the road.

'Maybe I should drive?'

'Are you worried?'

'Not really.' But she could feel his anxieties like an inspill of the bristling night. 'Look, I didn't mean what I said about your father. And don't worry about Franco. What else could we have done?'

'Kept out of it. Maybe that's the only way to have clean hands? I feel mine are red.'

His bulk beside her had the unyielding density of masculine distress: knotted and unreachable like a rolled-up hedgehog. Men got that way, she remembered from her father. They retreated and couldn't let things out. But after a while Neri started to.

'My father ...' he kept saying, musing and agonizing over his mistake. 'God, the harm I could have done him ...' As he reconstructed the imbroglio now, the cabinet minister's son had been framed as he himself had nearly been. Both sons were to have been used to destroy their fathers' faction of the ruling party. The cell to which the other son belonged – *his* name, Neri now recalled, was Enzo – had been wiped out. *That,* Neri's informant at the garage believed, was likely to mean that the police would now pin a number of unascribed crimes on the dead young men. Enzo would be implicated. Having fled the country would be seen as a confession of guilt. It looked badly for Guido's clients. The Communists too might be accused of collusion unless, by some deal behind the scenes, they bought off the prosecution. Possibilities were endless.

'Well, you're out of it. You did no harm,' Anne reminded him.

But the shadow of what might have been clung to Neri. He had hoped, he protested, to *help* Guido. 'Like the filial Aeneas carrying the aged Anchises on his back!' He laughed sourly. 'Instead – I nearly dropped him in it.'

'Neri, it's *over.*' Franco, one way or another, had been neutralized.

'I was a pawn. A blind pawn. It's a foul game. My father, mind you, is blind too. A blind knight, shall we say? Or bishop? Expendable. Everyone's expendable in Italy today.'

They were back on the *autostrada* and he let the car race along the smooth ribbon of road. Then, his thoughts shifting, he remarked: 'Sort of awful, Franco worrying about underwear.'

She agreed, then wondered why. Was it because terrorists were supposed to manifest the forces of History that one expected them to be impersonal? Nobody thought pigeon droppings took from the dignity of public statues, but rig these out with soap and a towel and they'd look ridiculous. It was the gap between public and private concerns. One couldn't see Judas or Brutus falling into it or anyone in the Ancient or Third World – or, come to think of it, many people in Ireland. In retrospect the slovenliness of some of the boys she'd known in college took on bravura. She wondered what Bonaccorso would make of this? Maybe those English nannies had sapped the spirit of his class? Finicky hygiene was neither godly nor heroic.

Neri talked about Franco. 'He seemed to think you were his wife!' he noted. 'Or girl friend. I don't even know if he's married. He wasn't a congenial guest. He was jumpy and the least thing could set him off.' Neri began to tell of how once Franco had glimpsed Anne and the *fattore*'s children playing croquet. 'He could only see part of the game because of the angle of his window and that infuriated him. He made a little speech about girls idling on green lawns. Full of social envy. "Here we have," he said, "that sweetness of life first mourned by Talleyrand which all revolutions are accused of sweeping away. It lingers in enclosures like this: overripe, a little rotten, but exquisite, melancholy and intense. You," he told me, "should be out there instead of here with me. You'll never do any good with politics. You probably won't do any harm either because you'll be ineffectual. You're irrelevant, Neri. Play croquet. It's your sort of game." Of course he was needling me, but I had an impression too that he would have liked to be playing croquet himself.'

'Odd for a revolutionary – or a policeman.'

'If we were clever, it might help us guess which he is,' said Neri. 'We're coming to a cafeteria. Shall we have a snack?'

'Yes.'

He pulled in and parked. Inside the cafeteria, bright, ugly lights were reflected from chrome and mirrors. Catching sight of himself in one of these, he became depressed. Sitting down at a table, he put his head in his hands.

'Shit, shit, shit, shit!'

Later, he remarked that the day's events would have amused his father who, like all good conservatives, liked to see life as a joke. Hadn't Anne noticed this, he heckled with mounting aggression.

'Look.' Neri took a yellowish newspaper clipping from his wallet. It was a photograph showing a group of men on a balcony. 'There's our last prime minister but two. There's my father's current client. The man on his right is now in a Swiss gaol facing charges of fraud. The one next to him, a banker with Vatican connections, was found hanged last year, possibly by those same connections, and there, on his other side, is my respected papa. I cherish this photo. It shows that he moves in a world of quick-change artists, a sort of circus. Jokes are useful there: a way of saying two things at once. Like Mussolini saying of his enemies: "I'll cap their teeth with gold. It will stop them biting." '

'Meaning he'd buy them off?'

'Yes. The joke made it appear cosy and acceptable. It also showed toughness since a man who caps teeth might pull them too.'

'You don't actually dislike Guido, do you?'

'I'm not sure. He humiliates me a bit. He's never taken me seriously. He's not a villain like those others but his ease in dealing with them upsets me. I suppose I find it hypocritical. Don't you find this balcony a good symbol? Imagine a man on a balcony covered with good things. A hungry man tries to climb up and get them but the man on top pushes him down. "I'll get you yet!" yells the hungry one. He's a revolutionary, you see. He's using rhetoric to keep his spirits up. "I'll settle your hash, you fat cat!" But the other one just laughs. That's the conservative's trick: laughter. It discourages the opposition. It also diminishes Left-Wingers who were once considered rather stylish. Romantic even. Nowadays, women prefer the suave chap who has the goods and tells jokes.'

'But that's your fate, Neri.'

'You think I'll end up like my old man?'

'Yes. He wasn't always so self-assured.' She began to tell him about Guido and her mother. Gossip had the kick of alcohol for her but, seeing that Neri was less taken with it, she broke off. 'Shall we go?' she suggested. 'I'll drive for a bit.'

Back on the *autostrada*, she felt him relax or perhaps sag.

'Your father,' she remarked, 'is attractive to us both. We both want to appropriate his attraction. Oh yes you do, Neri. That notion of yourself as Aeneas lifting the old man on your shoulders shows that.'

'Well, it's a less savage myth than Oedipus. *You* want to carry my father off too. Since you think I'm bound to become like him, why not marry me? Show confidence.'

'I might have to wait too long.'

Kilometres of pale motorway fled beneath their headlights relieved by the occasional red rear light and flash of a number plate: FI, BO, MI, Florence, Bologna, Milan. Then they left the *autostrada*, took some secondary and tertiary roads and were back at the villa. It was ten-thirty p.m.

'Remember to see Ida first and get her story.'

'Yes.'

Neri slid from the car and was off like a cat in the night. In her rear-view mirror there was no sign of him at all.

CHAPTER SEVEN

Driving into the courtyard, she noticed an unusual number of lighted windows. Ida's, however, was dark and there was no answer to Anne's knock on her door.

'Ida!' she called softly, and then less softly. 'Ida.'

'Signorina Anna!'

Across the courtyard, Bruni peered from a crack between two shutters. He gestured to her to come over and a moment later was unbolting a door.

'Where's the marchese?' he asked. 'The Signora Marchesa has been taken ill.' Bruni's head bobbed in the dimness like a parsnip simmering in broth. Peripheral parts of the villa were lit with the thriftiest electric light bulbs sold and could hardly have looked darker in the era of candles. There was a grey, leaky quality to the light from these sparse globes which hardly achieved any concentration of luminosity at all.

Bruni's question too had her in the dark. 'Do you mean Neri?' she wondered, although he was never given the title.

'*Macchè* Neri!' The parsnip head jiggled. 'No, no. I'm talking about the Marchese Guido. Ida said you were with him.'

'Oh, well, yes … but that was hours ago.' Anne hoped that this would not contradict whatever story Ida had told. Ida, she remembered too late, should have been warned of Niccolosa's fierce opposition to Anne's being out with Guido. 'Can I see her?'

'The marchesa? She's very ill.'

And probably very furious, thought Anne and for the second time that day felt red-handed. Being upset was alleged to be fatal to Niccolosa.

'I'll see if she'll see me,' she said.

The villa was feverish. A maid came dashing past.

'They've called the ambulance,' she said over her shoulder. 'We're to get her overnight bag ready on the double.'

'What's wrong with her?'

'The doctor doesn't know. Her temperature is thirty-nine point five.'

Ida, in ambush in an anteroom, was putting bottles into a medicine kit. She had been trying to contact the marchese all evening.

'You shouldn't have said I was with him.'

'No?' A spasm of intelligence clapped Ida's face tight. 'Well, we can't mend that now. Say you ran into him at the *antiquario*'s shop and drove off for a coffee. On your way someone rammed his car and the police held you both for questioning. Then you left him and went to look for the Lancia but you'd left it parked in front of someone's garage and they had it towed away. It took you until now to get back. You phoned here twice and spoke to me each time.' Ida, having dispensed this therapeutic lie – 'The bigger the more believable!' she advised – continued packing medicines into the pockets of the sealskin kit.

Niccolosa's room seethed in semi-darkness. A silk shawl had been thrown over a lamp. Maids poked through drawers, rejecting garments too bulky to be packed. Sounds from the bed suggested breathing difficulties.

'Signorina Anna, don't tire her.' One of them made a furtive gesture, tapping her own forehead. 'Delirious!' she mouthed.

Niccolosa's robust figure had lost gravity. She lay as if

beached and boned. Her mouth had fallen inwards and her flesh seemed to melt and spread. The eyes turned on Anne had the dark plasticity of boiling caramel.

'Anne!' she managed and a palsy played through rucked sheets. 'You should not ... not ... *not* ...' The force agitating her was preventing her getting sentences out. Her fingers worked on the sheet edge. She made a visible effort, took on consistency and focused her strained energies. '... *not* see Guido or be with him.' The voice was steady now. Niccolosa had regained control. 'The reasons are not frivolous, Anne. They are technical. It's better you not know them. For your sake and his. Believe me, they are pro-hibbbbb ...' She was panting now, shaking with the effort of getting her breath. '... bitive!' she brought out.

A blue light sliced in through the window, sweeping and resweeping the room. A maid, looking out, announced that this was the ambulance and that she could see two men getting out of it with a wheelchair. They'd be here to take the marchesa any moment.

Niccolosa ignored all this.

'I'm lucid,' she told Anne. 'Do you believe me?' The caramel eye boiled and caught the light. 'Truthfully? Will you give me your word? You're not in love with him, you know. It's a mis-apprehension. When I come back from hospital I'll tell you why. Give me your word to keep away from him until then.'

'All right,' said Anne. 'I will.'

'Truly?'

'Yes.'

Niccolosa relaxed. The frothing sheet fell back and was again cotton. 'Good,' she said. 'Good, you're a good girl. It's nothing fanciful, you know,' she added, getting nervous again. 'Not anything to do with the devil for whom I've never had much time. More with the world and the flesh which are quite enough to cope with. Give me your hand.'

Anne did. Niccolosa's soft, deliquescent ones held it for a moment and the sensation was as if Anne had thrust her own hand into hot dough.

The men with the wheelchair had now come in the door followed by the doctor who must have met them below. They unfolded it, covered it with a wrap and stood waiting.

'I'm afraid we must take her now,' said the doctor and gestured Anne away.

Niccolosa held on to her sleeve. 'Promise,' she croaked hoarsely.

'I promise.'

The doctor unclutched her fingers and Niccolosa was lifted into the chair.

'Send Guido,' she was ordering as they took her out. 'M-m-must talk with ... G-G-Guido.'

Carried aloft in her portable wheelchair, down the broad stairway like a Pope or prelate, Niccolosa was followed by Ida and the two maids with kits, wraps, grips and oddments some of which were rejected by the ambulance men and left like jetsam on the ground. The ambulance light caught the fountain jet, then the bust of a terracotta nymph on the corner of the terrace. Ida was going with Niccolosa, and Guido, when located, should be told to join them at the hospital. Anne must see to this.

'The phone numbers are by the library phone,' Ida reminded as she followed her patient into the ambulance. The doors were shut and it took off down the cypress walk, its light chopping at black-plumed trees.

Anne stood staring for some moments in its wake. How excessive people were, she marvelled. How they jay-walked through feeling! Niccolosa's appeal and her expenditure of self had left Anne tuned and tense. Accumulations of excitement dazed her, though she was conscious too that the sick woman was probably presenting something quite ordinary in terms magnified by her delirium.

What? What was it likely to be? Could Guido be selectively mad? Afflicted with some disease? Was he a Bluebeard? Of course not! A man with genital herpes then? An epileptic or schizophrenic? Surely such things could be *said*, if true? But if they had been true, Neri and his mother would have known of them – and *they* were not given to beating about the bush. Perhaps Niccolosa was simply and obsessively re-enacting the old story with Anne's mother? A sadly innocent little tale it seemed now. Anne had come on further details in the old letter given her by Maria-Cristina. In it, Mummy kept repeating what had clearly become a sweet-and-sour joke about Guido's failure to make love to her, comparing him to someone in Dante's hell-of-the-lukewarm who 'cravenly the great refusal made'. *Her* refusal years later in Dublin would have this earlier one behind it. Betrayal begot betrayal. Not that Niccolosa was likely to know about any of that. Her role in the thing had been short and speedy. She had caught the two kissing. Guido – there had been some domestic occasion for this, some disappointment not clarified in the letter – had told her 'We were just comforting each other.' And Niccolosa had given them a last chance. If from now on they behaved with propriety, she would not, she promised, send Anne's mother away. The promise, however, was half-hearted. 'Propriety' was not defined and Niccolosa was now on the warpath. The word 'comfort' had rankled with her and when, some days later, she came on the two listening to a record of the counter-tenor, Alfred Deller, singing Elizabethan songs, she took sharp exception to the words.

Anne turned from the cypress walk and made for the library. A lilt came to her lips. It was the Deller song which Mummy had continued to like and sing. How did it go? *Give me kind Amaryllis, the wanton country maid . . ./Her when we court and kiss, she cries: 'Forsooth, let go!'/But when we come where comfort is, she never will say 'No'.* That had clinched things for Niccolosa. 'Comfort' was an indecency. She had guessed as much when Guido first said it. Now she knew. Mummy was shown the door of the villa. 'Comfort' was out and so was she.

Anne laughed to herself. The old lady had always been one to make a mountain out of a molehill. No doubt she was doing so again.

Anne began to make phone calls to Guido. He was neither at the Florentine palazzo, the maritime villa nor at a number in Rome where he was supposed to be sometimes available. She left messages at all three places and was leaving the library when she heard a movement at the window.

It was no surprise to see Neri standing on the sill. The shutters, closed by day, would have been opened earlier in the evening to freshen the room then, presumably, forgotten in the excitement over Niccolosa.

A sky milky with stars hung above him. He could have been in a Tuscan painting, poised in one of those slim vistas opening on to the outer dark which were as much as the old artists cared to practise in the architecture of their canvasses. Incursions from without were guarded against as carefully as ebullitions of feeling within.

'I saw the ambulance.'

'Your grandmother has had some sort of crisis.'

'I was afraid of that. Do you think that's our fault? Mine for getting you back late and worrying her?'

He jumped down into the room and began to move restlessly about. She recognized her own ragged mood in his. 'I think I'm cursed,' he said. 'Worse: I think I carry a curse. I may have the evil eye.' Making a warding-off gesture with clenched fist and extended index and little finger, he turned this on himself, then held it between a lamp and a wall, throwing horned shadows. 'I've been listening to the radio,' he said. 'Enzo has turned up in Switzerland.'

'Who?'

'My father's client's son. Remember? The other son in the case.' He saw them now as twinned. 'He's refusing to speak to the press. I'm glad he's alive. I'd expected to hear he'd been shot crossing the border with drugs or something. Planted on him, naturally. But he beat them to it. My father will probably be going up there now to talk to him.' Neri paced about. 'Sorry. I'm babbling a bit. Remember that book I had here the first time we met? About our revolutionary ancestor? He turned out to be embarrassingly inept. What Franco would call a fuck-up. His efforts to keep Florence a republic ushered in three hundred years of ducal rule. I think I'm off politics. Action provokes reaction. What's the point?'

'The safe place to have learned that was school. Didn't they teach history at yours?'

'I didn't trust them. My father sent me to school to priests. "To give me moral vertebra." Imagine! All they taught was how to grow a conventional shell to make up for having no vertebra at all. The R C Church is one big, cosy mollusc shell. Naturally, *I* decided to be an individualist.'

'Maybe he planned it that way?'

'Maybe. Shall we have a drink? Nonna Niccolosa has some awfully good Armagnac.' Neri found glasses in a cupboard and poured for himself and Anne. 'Here's to her.' He raised his glass. 'How *is* she? How did she look?'

Anne told him.

Neri topped up their glasses. 'We're drinking too fast,' he reproved. 'I think that's typical of our generation. We should savour things more. For instance, you and I ought to savour each other. Don't I attract you at all, Anne? You attract me. Don't laugh. I'm serious tonight – and therefore miserable. I'm being educated at painful speed. You think I'm "young", don't you. Young for my years and light years younger than you who, to be sure, are stiff with female wisdom? Well, pity me for that.'

'I do pity you. You're under strain.'

A pulse began to quiver in Neri's neck just below the start of his jawline. He stared at the ceiling, then at his glass. 'That was a mistake,' he said. 'I might break down now. Weep. Disgrace myself. And pity is the enemy of love, isn't it? I'd like a little love.'

'You're getting like Guido. Love is his subject.'

'Has he a monopoly? Can't I replace him in your affections? Seriously, if you and I made a match, wouldn't that flout the beastly fates? Make up for my grandmother's mistake with your mother. I'll bet *she'd* favour it. She'd consider you good for me. You would be too.' Neri, raising his glass, considered its translucent glow. 'Old, old Armagnac,' he murmured with malice. 'That's how you see my father, I'll bet: as a smooth, great old vintage. But men aren't like alcohol. There are some vital differences to the way they age.'

'You're being vulgar.'

'Truth is vulgar. Wisdom is vulgar. Do you know the old saw: "When old men marry, the church bells toll the death knell"?'

'Neri, it has been a long day. May I lock you out?'

'Please.' His hand was on her arm. 'I don't think I can bear to be alone.'

'I'm not your nanny, Neri.'

'I should hope not.' Beguilingly: 'She *would* have left me alone.'

'For being bad?'

'Yes, but my intentions are good. Really. If I lack judgement it's because of my appalling childhood. Do you know that at my monstrous school we studied Greek, Latin, English, German and French as well as Italian and the usual other things? We never had a chance to just *be* and now we're all emotionally backward. It's the truth. Our feelings are like pet animals which have been caged up, then suddenly let out.'

'I don't think you let them out. I think you sometimes poke a finger into their cage and get bitten. But you haven't let them out.'

'How brilliant you are! I *need* to talk like this. You're exactly what I need, Anne. I love you.'

'No: you're *thinking* of loving me.'

They laughed: a quivering fit of joint mirth which kept starting again each time it had seemed to die down. She supposed they were a bit light-headed.

'You're thinking of *practising* love on me,' she added, taken by the game.

He sat beside her on the couch. 'We laugh too much,' he said soberly. 'Actually, it's not true about my feelings. They're quite strong. It's just that I can't disentangle them. Am I boring the hell out of you?'

'No, but,' she decided to admit, 'I keep imagining I see the young Guido in you: floundering, generous, a bit lost. The one my mother knew. So *I'm* playing too. You'll agree that that's fair.'

'Oh Christ! Guido, Guido, Guido, Guido!'

'Maybe you should go away somewhere?' she suggested. 'Get over him.'

'I want *you* to get over him.'

'You don't really care about me. You're interested in me because of him.'

'No.'

'Yes.'

'You mean you're Jocasta? My surrogate mother?'

'You read too many books.'

'Well, I've read them now. I can't just forget them, can I? I mean whatever I do or think of doing has probably been done with more style by someone in a book – or by bloody

Guido. If I didn't *know* it mightn't matter. But I do. I suppose that's what it means to be decadent? Images and shadows get in the way of reality. But *you* attract me, Anne. Really. I swear. Be honest enough to stop pretending you don't know.'

'All right,' said Anne. 'I attract you. You attract me. But lots of people are attractive. It doesn't mean much. You're a chameleon, Neri. I couldn't fall in love with you.'

'Because I play roles? But I hate that. I want to stop.'

'Maybe the best way would be to play a role so hard it became real.'

'That's what I want to do with you.'

'Right. Let's make it interesting. Give me up.'

'I'd have to *have* you first, wouldn't I? But, seriously, falling in love with an older man is a folly. It's an effort to appropriate the past *as it was*. It can't be done, *cara*. Better a live dog, they say, than a dead lion. Better a young Neri than an old Guido. It's not like buying a brand name, you know. You don't get something fresh made to an old recipe. You're more in the position of Antony taking the cold morsel from Casear's plate when he fucked Cleopatra. That's old wisdom.'

'Words, words, words.'

'*I'm* ready for acts, acts, acts. Are you?'

'No.'

Teasing the handsome Neri was like playing with a lion cub. The mature male was there in embryo. The claws could scratch. The bouncy suppleness amused, touched – and put her off. It wasn't the suppleness of an adult. Neither were his sulks – or were they? If I hadn't know Guido, she thought, who knows?

But comparison was in Guido's favour.

'Once,' she counselled gravely, 'I used to be like you, wanting so hard to feel things that I never could. We're no good for each other. You'll have to find someone who anchors you the way Guido does me.'

'What a rotten trick!' he exclaimed. 'You take my one obvious asset, my youth, and turn it into a drawback. Why do I let you? I won't have it. *Gaudeamus igitur* – why aren't we singing and dancing?'

'No music.'

'Wrong, *cara*, wrong!' He moved a panel and revealed a phonograph and a stack of records. 'I'll put on something old-hat, syrupy and reeking of *vita brevis*.'

'Suppose someone hears?'

'Who? Bruni? The maids? They don't matter. We have the place to ourselves.'

'I can't do that – what is it? A foxtrot?'

'*Senti, bella*, you'll have to make do with what you find. Do you expect my grandmother to have reggae? These are probably the records your mother danced to.' He had put on '*Nel blu dipinto di blu*', threaded his arms through hers and begun guiding her with neat, tidal movements to and fro around the floor, tracing a pattern as simple as a knitting motif or the design on an ancient Roman tile. '*Nel blu dipinto di blu,*' sang Perry Como, '*Felice di stare qua su.*' His voice mesmerized them with the sugary simplicities of their parents' youth. '*Vol-a-a-are, oho oho ò! Canta-a-are, oho oho ò!*' The sounds soared and swooped.

'Anne, don't you think we might comfort each other a little?'

The word startled her. 'Where did you get that word?'

'What word? What's wrong with it, Anne? Mmm? What's wrong with a little comfort?' He breathed delicately into her ear. 'Hm?'

'Mmmm.' Almost of its own volition, she felt her mouth fasten on his.

Lips locked, eyes shut, they slid to the floor. The record

came to an end and the turntable continued silently to spin.

'Anne.'

She opened her eyes.

Neri's voice was urgent. 'Wake up. Hurry.'

A grainy, greyish light was oozing in and for moments she had no idea where she was, nor even that the dim rectangle above her was a window. Its luminescence had the sluggish hesitancy of the sea flooding a cave. Neri, however, was shaking her and she saw that this was the library and that she must have slept on the hearthrug.

'Put your clothes on,' he told her, 'that's my father's car in the drive. He'll be here in a minute.'

'Jesus, what time is it?'

'Four a.m.'

She was covered with mosquito bites. One had swollen her eyelid. She rubbed this.

'Hurry,' Neri harried her. 'He mustn't know about this. He couldn't cope.'

Neri had pulled on his jeans and was tucking in his shirt. He dipped his handkerchief in soda water and rubbed it over his face, ran his fingers through his hair, then turned to help her. 'Here.' He handed her the gold-thonged sandals, straightened a lock of her hair and whispered, 'Put them on. Don't say anything. I'll talk.' He was like a wound spring.

Guido was in the hall. They heard him open a door on the side which led to the kitchens, then approach their own. Neri switched off the turntable, and placed himself at some distance from Anne.

'You came down because you heard a noise,' he whispered. 'You were in bed. Then you threw on your clothes and came down and caught me here – like that first time. OK?'

The door opened.

Guido stood in the doorway. There was a feeling of something breaking rhythm: a hitch, an indrawn breath.

'Well ... hullo.'

His face was stiff. 'I saw the shutter open, so I came to investigate.' He spoke with a casualness too sustained to be true. Perhaps he felt this for he added: 'I didn't know you two knew each other.' There was neither curiosity in his voice nor a natural surprise. 'But then why should I? After all I'm here so little.' He managed a smile. Clearly, he wouldn't interrogate them and, given the oddness of the circumstances, his restraint too was odd. For the first time, Anne saw fragility in him and some strain and it struck her that he must have come from the hospital and had perhaps been up all night. She opened her mouth to speak but Neri got in before her.

'We *don't* know each other,' he told his father. 'Or rather the worst is now known about *me* who, I'm afraid, have been caught burgling. I came in the window.' He gestured towards it with a pirouette. 'That's why the shutter's open.'

Guido's face was mistrustfully polite. 'At this hour?'

'Well, it *is* the burglar's hour.' His son spoke with some swagger. 'Actually, I'd only intended taking a book, but I must have made rather a lot of noise. I disturbed a guest.' He gestured at Anne. 'I've already apologized.'

She couldn't look in his direction, but was aware of him running through one of his mime routines. His tone just now had been cheeky and insufferable.

Guido turned to her. 'You came down alone to confront...?'

'... an intruder,' Neri cut in. 'Yes, but it was only me. I'm a gentle burglar. *Vero, Signorina?*' he appealed to Anne. 'Isn't it true that I am? *Gentile*, even?'

Guido shouted suddenly. 'Stop clowning, you little bastard.'

'*Am* I one?'

Anne longed to shout 'cut' like a film director. But she wasn't in control here. The situation had its own impetus.

'Your grandmother is dying,' Guido harangued his son, 'and you seize the chance to rifle her possessions. What's the matter with you? What values do you live by? Have you no moral sense?'

'How could I have?' Neri demanded. 'Your generation loves those words! You suck them like sweets. You melt them to a meaningless goo. How can someone my age use them after you?'

'What were you *doing* here, Neri?'

'Burgling. I came for a book.'

'I don't understand you.'

'I know.' Neri gave his father a grin. He had slid into sincerity, but was backing from it like a scalded creature. She had been wrong in thinking the situation out of control. Neri was directing it and did not intend having the showdown with his father which they would have to have one day soon. Not now. Neri's aim *now* was to present himself as an adolescent pest – Guido's view of him anyway – so as to deflect any suspicion that he might have become a sexual rival.

Anne, on the pretext of fastening the shutters, turned her hot face away from both men.

'I suppose I *am* a moral cretin,' she heard Neri say.

It was easier to look at him than at Guido and when she did she saw that his pose – one knee bent, denimed legs poised with the nonchalance of an Elizabethan coxcomb – made him look a lout. Seeing each with the other's eyes was unpleasant. What Guido couldn't know was that Neri was sacrificing his pride to save his father's. This was unexpectedly imaginative of Neri. Guilt over the Franco episode must have alerted him to Guido's way of seeing things. Without it, she doubted if it would have struck him that the carnal play in which he and she had indulged would matter to anyone. It had been friendly; it had been fun and engaged on with full agreement as to its lack of importance for their deeper selves.

Their generation probably took such comforts much as Guido's had kissing and as Niccolosa's might have viewed a couple going for an unchaperoned row in a boat.

Anne didn't regret it at all.

What she disliked was the complicity which made Guido look like a child or a fool from whom such things had to be kept. They did have to be. She recognized that and hated it. Neri and she, just when they should have been free of each other, were bound by scruple. It was ironic: concern for Guido's feelings was forcing them to lie to him. Impossible simply to tell the unimportant truth. Guido would make too much of it. He would suffer and this, she supposed, must mean that somebody's judgement was at fault. Probably it was hers and Neri's – after all, they hadn't shown much in the Franco episode, had they? No, considering the shambles they'd made of that, they should steer clear of situations in which people could get hurt. Feeling responsible and clumsy – it was like being back in Mummy's sickroom – she saw that it wasn't Guido but Neri and she who were the children here, then, with relief, saw too that this let them off the hook, for how could children's actitivies lie on the conscience? They couldn't. Making love with Neri had been inconsequential and in no way that mattered could be construed as an infidelity to Guido. She was thinking of *him*, it came to her, as men used to think of certain women. He was the 'good', i.e. marriageable mate who reinforces a weaker one's better self.

The casuistry in this argument only made it more compelling. Guido would give her backbone and in him she would find the honey of the past. No injudicious truth-telling must be allowed to jeopardize this.

'You *are* a moral cretin!' she heard and was startled. But he was talking to Neri.

'Please,' she begged, 'don't quarrel. Nothing happened,

after all. Nothing that matters.' Then – since this was dis-
courteous to Neri – 'And I've enjoyed meeting your son.' A
world where lies were unnecessary had come to seem remote.

'Get out!' Guido told Neri who gave Anne a theatrical little
bow, reopened the shutters and left through the window.

Guido walked to it, stood for some moments looking out,
then turned, sighed, shook his head and said: 'Fatherhood!
God! There goes my son and heir.'

'He's charming.'

'You can't mean it.'

'I think you rub each other the wrong way. He was perfectly
sweet until you came.'

'When I saw you together just now I was jealous.' Guido
spoke in a dogged voice as though Neri's quicksilver poses
had made him see himself as leaden and unable to compete.

She marvelled: 'Of *him*?'

'Don't you find him handsome?'

'Of course! He's so like you!' Nature, Guido had said the
other evening, endows lovers with its resources. Anne felt
endowed. She could feel her voice lilt with seductive gaiety
and her smile must be like a lamp.

'And young.'

'A boy. A sketch for the real thing. A St John crying in
the wilderness: "Prepare ye the way of the Lord, make straight
his paths!"' The erotic come-on only became clear to her as
she spoke and seemed to be another of Nature's cues or hints.
She laughed, brazenly, sure she couldn't go wrong.

'The Irish blaspheme, don't they?'

'Like all Christians. Didn't *you* say that Florentine thinkers
believed men could be gods?'

'Did I?'

She saw that there was a darkness in him, a dragging gloom.
'There's something the matter, isn't there?' she asked.

As Neri had done earlier, Guido now began to pace and

shuffle about the library. He frowned and it was clear that some undertow in his feelings was coming to the fore.

He stopped in front of her. 'I'm in a quandary,' he explained. 'You see my mother is dying. There's no longer any doubt of that. Not today nor tomorrow, perhaps, but, well, to come out with it, I suspect that what Neri was doing here was looking for a will. That was why I lost my temper. I suppose I must have seemed mad ... Bear with me, Anne. I've been up all night. It's five a.m. and I've got professional pressures too. Crises. I'll have to leave almost at once for Switzerland. Meanwhile, here, everything seems ...' He passed a hand over his face and managed to smile but there was no serenity in him. 'My head,' he apologized, 'is a jumble of love, money and suspicion. My mother is behaving oddly and my wife thinks that this is because you brought pressure on her. My son is most probably my wife's spy and I can't bear for any of this to come between us.'

'Why? How?' But of course she saw that his family's suspicion of her could poison things. It had an insidiousness with which it was hard to come to grips and, remembering the monsignor's hints, had been there, latent and dormant from the first. Suspicious in turn, she was half disposed to believe that Neri had indeed been looking for a will – and maybe keeping an eye on her. Could he have kept her out late so as to get her in trouble with Niccolosa? No, Neri was an idealist. Look how he had behaved just now with Guido. Surely he couldn't at the same time have been trying to foil any hopes she might have of pocketing some of his family's money?

'Anne.' Guido gave her a beseeching look. He sighed.

Some of the sigh was for her, she supposed. But not all. Far from it. Just now she had been on the point of falling into her mother's old delusion whereby love determined the pattern of events. Foolish, Anne, foolish! Love was like a pilot light in a domestic stove. It could leap into flowery flame and warm and burn up. But usually, it was not let. Pyromaniacs were put away. People with tendencies like that were shunned. Love's scope was limited. If you forgot this, you tended to give the wrong responses and get the wrong end of the stick.

She wanted to stroke his cheek but was held back by a fear that she might smell of Neri.

He sighed again, but was probably on the track of money rather than sex. A lawyer, his senses might tingle at the presence of guilt, then misdiagnose it. Her mood, infected by his, had taken a dive. Did *he* suspect her of money-lust? She thought it the meanest human impulse but, judging by everyone else's concern with it, must be wrong. Still she longed to yell: 'Guido, it's plain lust only that's been having play here. Is that so terrible? Neri and I were *lonely*. Your mother had put me off you, set up doubts. I was needy and where were you? Don't think I'm mercenary, Guido. I haven't been coveting your ox and your ass, only making a bit free with your son. You're on the wrong scent, sniffing out the wrong sin – and you don't want to know about it, anyway, Guido. It was nothing. It doesn't count. Let Neri and me pay the tribute of our hypocrisy to your virtue – you surely don't want to be told?'

Which meant she had nothing to say at all.

'I have to talk business for a bit,' said Guido gloomily.

'Business?'

'Yes.' He paused, then said briskly: 'My mother tells me that she plans to leave this villa to you in her will.'

'I'm sorry. Can you say that again.'

He did.

'Is this some sort of test?' In her mind possibilities organized themselves into one: this is (a) a joke; (b) mad; (c) dangerous. Tick one only. Or was Niccolosa tempting Anne to trade love for money? This seemed possible. Guido had just described his own mind as being full of both. Were they in opposition? Convertible? Or had his mother, eager, at the end, to shed her earthly assets, family pride included, chosen to bestow them on Anne as being the nearest equivalent of the beggar at the gate?

'Possibly,' said Guido, 'it is a test of *me*. She has asked me not to contest this legacy as my family would normally expect me to do. Grounds would be that she has known you under a month and can't be in her right mind. That you have no claim and must have exerted undue pressure. We would win. Wait.' He held up a hand. 'Please. *I* don't believe this, but you've got to know it.'

Beggar at the gate, thought Anne. Interloping daughter of an interloper. Pest. Vulture. Crow. From the start, Niccolosa's reasons for inviting her had been ambiguous.

'You say "we would win". You needn't worry. There won't be a contest. Your mother must be delirious. This can't be a serious move.'

'It is, though. She drew up the will just after you got here.'

'I don't want anything.'

'Please, Anne, there's no point getting upset. Try to remember that you're talking to two people: the Guido who loves you and the one who has a duty to his family . . .'

'I don't . . .'

'Listen, will you? *I* can see how my mother came to this decision. I think your mother's death and Flavia's have fused in her mind. Remember you came here on the day of Flavia's funeral. Well, anxiety about the past must have taken on distressing proportions. She's trying to set something right retroactively. I wouldn't say she's *non compos mentis*, but . . .'

'I don't *want* the legacy!'

'*Please* hear me out. There need be no litigation. The thing can be managed amicably. We can make a contract dividing it between us. I owe it to Neri to do this and . . .'

'I don't want any part of it.'

'You must take half.'

'Why?'

'It's only right. In deference to her. I have other assets. There's nothing disgraceful about gifts or ownership, Anne.'

'Look, she's made me look a gold-digger!' And of course *that* was Niccolosa's strategy! Since the legacy was so easy to contest, it was a risk-free way of uniting the family – all those needy-looking aunts – against Anne and, eventually, turning Guido too against her. Like a slow-working poison, the move might have already begun to pay off.

He had begun to protest and perorate, begging her not to be needlessly proud. *He* knew, after all, that she wasn't a gold-digger, surely she knew that? 'Time ran out on my mother,' he pleaded. 'That's why this awkwardness has come into the thing. But we can straighten it out. She's making the only gesture of conciliation that it is open to her to make towards you, your mother and the past. She's giving you a freedom which your mother never had. Take it, Anne. Later, not now – now I don't want you to answer me – I'll ask you to think about marrying me. We must keep that a separate issue. I had to tell you about the legacy now because I have to be away for a day or so – I have to go to Switzerland on this wretched case – and my mother is liable to want to see you before I get back. I had to prepare you. But it would be as well *not* to let her know that I've suggested you sign half of it away. It is to ensure your being able to hold on to the other half that I advise this. Otherwise, my wife might sue you for the lot. I'm advising you as a lawyer now.'

'Oh Guido, the shifts and shuffles!' Anne sighed wonderingly. *Could* Niccolosa have wanted her to have the property? It was hard to believe. Kin was her prime value. Property went to kin. It seemed likelier that she had marked

Anne down for destruction by her poisoned gift. Yet, Anne couldn't quite believe this either.

'That's how societies work,' Guido was saying. 'And the family is a small society. There are always contracts when people marry ...'

'You are married!'

'Hardly, you know. Hardly at all. I think my wife will be relieved to divorce. But I don't want you to say how you feel about marrying me yet. Think about it. Sleep on it. I'd rather you took time to decide.'

'About which? Marriage or the legacy?'

'Both. I'll phone you from Switzerland. And remember: in life, to get by at all, one has to compromise.'

'And sometimes lie?'

'Oh we *must* lie to my mother. It's only kind.' Mistaking her expression, he added: 'Don't be shocked. Just remember who the non-compromisers are in our society. The terrorists ...'

'Terrorists?' Could he have found out about Franco?

'Indeed! Think where non-compromise has led *them*.'

'Where? Which ones? Has something happened?'

'Oh love, you're sleepy. Fuddled. You were woken up by my beastly son and now I'm facing you with major decisions. I'm sorry.' He kissed her. 'And boring you with my professional burdens. This case ...' He sighed.

How selfish I am, she thought. He's being pressured on all sides. She hugged and felt him slack and a little bowed within her embrace. He kissed her heavily and slowly, as though sealing her, she thought, making a ritual of it, a kind of promise. For a moment she felt the strain of his sadness begin to mingle with her own mood, but then, looking over his shoulder towards the window, saw this begin to lighten, for the dawn was starting: a bright, giddy, summer dawn so that the sky was no longer grey but a deep, rich gold with feathery tatters of red scattered and, in some cases, clustered against it like flocks of red-winged cupids on a gilded panel.

Siesta time – but nobody in the villa was taking a siesta. Timetables were being ignored as though the expectation of death had made time intolerable.

Ida, a harbinger, was back from the hospital with news of the poor marchesa who was being martyrized by doctors but had rebelled.

'They wanted to cut into her to do tests – and what for? If she's dying, what for? They've done enough cutting.' An abscess in the old lady's stomach had been drained and now she was on the mend. 'It was like pregnancy,' said Ida. 'She was swollen up as if she were nine months pregnant.'

She and Anne were in the kitchen eating chilled water-melon. Emerald-skinned, its pulp had the texture of crushed snow and was sweet and red with bright spanglings of ice water. *Popone*. The rounded vowels suggested a baby at the breast. Anne, who had got up late, was treating this as brunch.

'She said she'd rather die than stay there and who'd blame her?' Ida was shocked by the ironing out of distinctions practised in the hospital. She had been prevented from minis-tering to the marchesa according to habits built up over fifty years. Doctors were elusive. Nurses threw their weight around. 'Bossy!' she complained. '*Prepotenti!*' The chauffeur was taking her back to spend the night with the Signora Marchesa. 'I wouldn't leave her alone with *them*! I just came here to get a few little things she needs. Then, tomorrow, we'll bring her home. I hear the Signor Conte dropped by. What did he say?' she wanted to know, eager to bring this scrap of homage to Niccolosa along with her street clothes and gloves for wearing in bed.

Anne had run into Bonaccorso shortly before Ida's arrival.

He had been in the library where, over a glass of medicinally fortifying brandy, he had talked mistily and angrily of love.

'He said,' she recalled, 'that life was a cheat and that it was better not to have lived if one had to die, nor to have friends if one must lose them.' Bonaccorso had poured forth these sentiments along with a stew of others which made less sense to her. Then he had stomped off to his car which he drove erratically and rowdily down the drive.

'How did he look?'

'Red in the face. He had two brandies while he was here.'

'Drinking!' said Ida with approval. 'Going to pieces. He's fond of her. Always was!'

Anne whistled in imitation of the old count. 'Phuitt!' she whistled. 'Life is a sell. *Un cattivo scherzo!* Here today and gone tomorrow. *Comme les hirondelles, ma chère!* Life is a trick, a cheat, a bad joke. If you can't seize today, reach out for yesterday. Live in your memory. *Pogue mahone.*'

Ida laughed. 'I'll tell the marchesa,' she decided. 'That will cheer her up.'

'How ill *is* she?'

Ida shrugged. 'Low. Jumpy. Repeats questions. Perhaps she doesn't hear?'

Anne imagined a grey-on-grey flight-information chart interminably rippling in a departure lounge: Niccolosa's brain. The image, it came back to her, was the old lady's own. Hadn't she compared what was left of her life to time spent waiting for a last flight to be called? This suggested that Niccolosa's view of things might well be no more wavery than the things themselves. It confirmed Anne's suspicion that the legacy was designed to put Guido off herself. The device didn't seem to be working but that didn't prove that Niccolosa hadn't hoped it might. Guilt, like the bats and tatters of evening, seemed to hover. It had to do with Anne's promise to keep away from Guido. If Niccolosa was not *non compos* then promises to her should perhaps be kept. Well, Guido, by now, was well on his way to Zurich. No need, for the moment, to think about that.

'I brought the papers from Florence,' said Ida and handed them to Anne who, taking them outside, sat on the fountain rim, cooling her hands in weed-green water. The sculpted dolphin, arrested in his leap for five hundred years, had gone nowhere but had gathered moss. A lozenge of yellow stucco fell across the water surface. In the depths moved a sly, decorative fish. Watching it, she forgot to read the provincial news to see if there was any mention of Franco.

CHAPTER EIGHT

It was the following evening.

'God is a swindler!'

Bonaccorso had spent thirty minutes with Niccolosa and was lingering in the room next to hers where Ida had set up a trolley with sandwiches and soup. Reluctant to leave, he poured himself a bowl of this, then forgot about it. The doctor had told him he couldn't see the dying woman again. Shortly after getting home, she had taken a turn for the worse and mightn't last until morning. Weeping, the count paced the area between the couch on which the monsignor had decided to spend the night and a card table on which Anne was eating a plate of spaghetti which Bruni had brought especially for her.

'Eat!' he'd said, plonking it in front of her. 'Everyone must eat.'

Bonaccorso paused in front of God's representative, the monsignor, and harangued him. 'Everything,' he whispered in a hiss of fury, 'is left just long enough for us to get used to it – and *then* withdrawn. Youth first. That's God's first dirty trick – assuming that he exists at all, which is another question. Tsssts!' Bonaccorso's animal sounds were tauter than usual. His lips guillotined the words as they emerged. 'Youth is an ocean to the young. You swim in it. It's all around you and bears you up. Then one day, tsssts, it's gone. Phuitt! Just like that! You're a marooned sea animal. Got to breathe air all of a sudden!' The count turned, paced, returned. 'Nobody accepts *that* without pain,' he said. 'Do you know about the old Tuscan shepherds who used to suck off the sperm of their young companions in the hope of getting their youth with it? The elixir of life, ha!' Another turn. More pacing. 'Do you believe that story?' he asked the monsignor. 'I believe it. I read it decades ago in a book by, I think, Giovanni Commisso, but I believe it. Someone must have told it to him. It has the ring of truth. Yes, yes. If there's a God he's evil. He must be. He gets us used to youth, love and life then, when they have come to seem our very elements, removes them. Why would a good God do that?' he asked.

The monsignor, whose religion, after all, had dealt fairly exhaustively with questions like this, chose not to reply. Instead, he made himself a sandwich from the food on the trolley and took a large, gagging bite. Chewing, he sat fat and silent like an idol until his sheer impassiveness and the regular movement of his jaws began to seem like an answer in themselves. He was demonstrating a natural process: eating, swallowing, existing. There was no arguing with this nor with death either. As to more metaphysical matters, he might have been doubting their usefulness to the count.

Anne wound spaghetti round her fork. The monsignor chewed. The count paced, stopped, paced again.

'Love,' he told them, 'is the worst cheat because choice seems to be involved. One doesn't *have* to love, after all. It's a purely self-inflicted pain.'

'Or pleasure?' suggested Anne.

'Pleasure,' Bonaccorso argued, biting his words off, syllable by syllable, 'is fi-nite. Plea-sure is *safe*. But love . . .'

The monsignor ate. Anne wound spaghetti and rewound it, then smuggled some into her mouth. She felt ashamed of her appetite. Bonaccorso paced and paused and pondered. He might have been doing the Stations of the Cross. 'One invests it with too much,' he stated. 'More than it will bear.' Looking back on his life, he said, he thought of love as a tucked-away memory like a magazine pull-out. Ordinary pages flicked by but this was three-dimensional. A special thing.

'Do you really mean a pull-out?' Anne wondered. 'As in *Playboy* Magazine?'

'You're an insolent young woman!' raged the count and had to be calmed. His anger was excessive and its excess became obvious even to him. 'Sorry,' he decided. 'Sorry.' It had meanwhile been clarified that he meant not a pull-out but a pop-up: one of those cut-outs in children's books – fairy castles or perhaps the House-that-Jack-Built – which leap into pretty erection when the page is opened. 'Frail! Magical!' lamented the count and jerked an elbow towards Niccolosa's room. 'I loved *her*,' he said, 'since I was sixteen. Fifty years, can you believe that? And never got closer than the occasional waltz. My hand on her bare back at decorous dancing parties. When I was eighteen I could dream about a dance like that for weeks. Once I stole a glove of hers which held her scent for half a year. Maybe I only thought it did? I used to dance with her twice, three times if I was in luck. Never more at any one party. I was too ... oh ... inconsistent. Slight. She liked men of energy. Guido talks about the best mates getting the best women. That's a vulgar idea. The louder, pushier ones do – but they're not best for love. Oh, in a sense maybe he's right. It's Nature improving her stock. Like a farmer, Nature doesn't care for subtlety. Breeders aren't concerned with love. I know. I used to be one. Tssts! Look at the societies which produce erotic art. Look who appreciated it. Lazy, courtly men, not warriors. Not heroes of Labour or the stock exchange. Niccolosa married a practical fellow. I doubt if he gave her much pleasure ...'

'Why should he?' The monsignor sliced a gherkin and

laid it in a plane on a slice of red beef. 'It's not the aim of marriage. Neither Nature nor Society benefits from means becoming ends. Pleasure is meant to be fleeting. The flower fades so that the plant may nourish the . . .'

'Fruit!' Bonaccorso cut in rudely. 'Parish sermon number what?'

The monsignor bit into his sandwich.

'Sorry,' said Bonaccorso and started to drink his cooled broth. 'The human condition,' he told the other two, 'is barely bearable here in the garden of Italy, so what must it be like elsewhere? I do see why religion was invented. I wish it worked for me – or that I could believe in some damn thing. Human perfectibility? How can one? I believe in the passing moment, yet never grasped it. Wish I had now. If I'd lived for pleasure I'd have bright memories. Pop-ups.' He giggled suddenly, then stopped just as suddenly so that the laughter had the rough abruptness of a sob. 'Remember that,' he told Anne. 'Accumulate good memories. Everything else is shit, pretence, danger even, as you'll learn soon enough. Like the revolutionaries who want to teach us how to live by blowing us up with their bombs. Boom! Did you read about that young man whose head was practically shot off by a hunter yesterday morning? Hm? Not far from here. A fugitive from the police – but the hunter thought he was a lark or partridge. Life is a poor joke. I'm not fit company. I'd better go. I'll be back in the morning. Get them to phone me if there's any change before then.'

Wiping his eyes with a large, lawn handkerchief, Bonaccorso stumbled from the room. They heard him clatter unsteadily down the stairs.

'He's quite sober,' said the monsignor, speaking at last. 'Just angry.'

'Grieving,' said Anne.

'No. Not yet. Anger is a defence against grief. He's a mild

man. I wonder if he ever let his anger rip before? He's a good farmer, you know, improves his land. Plants vines, olives – and for whom? *He'll* never see the fruit of them. But instinct is powerful in him. It's his own instinct he was raging at just now. Well, rage could bring him to religion yet.' The monsignor poured himself a glass of wine. 'Want some?' he asked Anne.

'Thanks.'

'*You're* next to see her.' The monsignor looked inquisitively at Anne. He had already annointed Niccolosa and had perhaps heard about the legacy. 'The family should be along soon. Ida tells me she got hold of them all on the phone, including Guido who's on his way back from Switzerland.' He sighed. 'It will be a long night. Do you think someone in the kitchen might think of making coffee?'

'I'll go and ask.' She was glad of the pretext to escape his curiosity.

Running downstairs she felt her hand touch the textured surface of a wall and, before she knew it, had stopped on a midway landing to look the place up and down. You did not yearn for what you couldn't hope to have any more than most people were able to think in very large sums, although bankers could, no doubt, covet by the billion. Anne knew that her mother's house in Dublin might fetch £75,000 – so *there* was a unit she could use. Perhaps the price of a single painting in the hall below her would buy that house? And vice versa. As though the figure were a pair of gigantic and predatory pincers, she turned it mentally on the furnishings and told herself: I could *buy* that table, the predella above it and maybe the *cassone* too. Vandalized, her image of the place became ravaged with holes. Then, she saw it once more as it was. Walls were hung with wine-red damask. Sheer looming space and the bulking shadows thrown by inadequate lamps made it all alien to her idea of comfort and she was soothed to see that she did not in fact covet it at all. Yet Niccolosa, like Satan, had, for whatever purpose, taken her to the mountain top to show her property and infect her with desire. Probably even the visit to the antiquarian's shop had been a move in the old woman's plan.

On her way back from the kitchens, she bumped into Neri who had just come in.

'Have you heard the news?' was his greeting. They hadn't met for a day and a half.

'About your grandmother?'

'No. About Franco.' Neri looked rumpled and distraught. His eyes were bloodshot and his face drawn into clusters of knots.

'What?' But she had guessed. Earlier, when Bonaccorso had talked of a terrorist being shot like a partridge, she had felt a shiver of half-knowledge, an anticipatory chill while managing, simultaneously, to not acknowledge what she knew. Maria-Cristina had said that living with lies was like walking through smoke. You used special apparatus. You filtered things out.

'He was found shot in the head.' Neri's words confirmed her guess like a caption or subtitle. In the head, she thought, oh God! The dead body of her own father, which they had not let her see, mixed into the image like bits of a cubist painting. Fractured. Chopped. Too many limbs. Blown apart. Shot in the head. Somewhere a girl called Mariuccia was waiting.

'At close quarters,' said Neri. 'Some miles from where we left him. It was in the papers. I thought you must know.'

'Could it,' she tried to hope, 'have been an accident?'

Neri unfolded a copy of *Paese Sera.* Yesterday's. 'Read it yourself.'

She followed his finger to the headline, HUNTER MIS-

TAKES PANAMA HAT FOR BIRD IN BUSH. The text ran,
'In the early hours of this morning in the Val d'Orcia,
Signor Gianni Datini, a local sportsman, saw what looked
like a fluttering of wings in a juniper bush and took aim ...
"This tragedy," said this prominent and respected citizen of
Pienza, "has destroyed my pleasure in the sport for all time."
So shattered was he by the experience that he had to be rushed
to hospital along with his victim who was pronounced dead
on arrival.'

'How do we know it was Franco?'

'The later editions had his identity.'

'I see.'

'He hadn't got a hat,' Neri reminded her.

'God! But this Datini sounds genuine. How can it have
been set up?'

'How could it not have been? Why would Franco be hiding
in a juniper bush in open country at six a.m. wearing a panama
hat? He should have been in a hospital bed. Whoever did
it was efficient. It happened only hours after we dropped him
off. I feel like the respected citizen: responsible.'

'Neri, don't blame yourself. Franco played with fire.'

'Don't let me off the hook, Anne. I'm taking this as a
sign ...'

She was too shaken to listen to his maunderings. Smoke,
she thought. We walk through smoke. Well, we should be
careful not to hurt each other, shouldn't we? Neri was saying
that though he was not so arrogant as to think Fate had killed
Franco so as to bring him to his senses, he couldn't ignore
the lesson and ... My God, she thought, how narcissistic
young men are!

'I'm a trouble-source,' said Neri. 'I could have made trouble
between you and my father too,' he castigated himself,
'though I wasn't serious and you both *are*. I saw that the
moment he came in the door.'

'You did no harm.'

'But I *might* have. When I say I wasn't serious about you, I meant I haven't it in me to be. There was something about the two of you when he walked in and stood there like, oh, a block of pain that showed me my own . . .'

Again she stopped listening, then, after a while, heard him ask about his grandmother and whether Anne had talked to her yet.

'Not yet. No. She's recovering from talking to Bonaccorso.'

They went upstairs where Neri made himself a sandwich and began talking to the monsignor who, Anne gathered, had prepared him years ago for confirmation. Her mind drifted and when she listened again Neri was talking about a priest he knew, one of his former teachers, who was doing social and pastoral work in a rural slum in Ecuador in the diocese of the Red Bishop of Riobamba. Neri was thinking of volunteering to work there for a year. The particular village where his old teacher worked was on the slopes of a volcano. 'A volcano on the equator,' he enthused, 'doesn't it sound like a location Dante might have used in hell? The hell of the unstable perhaps? Or the irresponsible!'

Ida came to say that the marchesa was ready to see Anne.

'Don't argue with her,' she whispered. 'She's very weak.'

She left Anne alone with the old woman who, lying inert against her pillows, looked nearly dead already. Her age spots seemed damp, darker than usual and could have been spatterings of fresh clay.

'Anne. Come over. Take my hand.'

Anne did. Bending in, she caught a sour whiff of decrepitude as she held the limp extremity.

'The monsignor,' said Niccolosa, husbanding her forces and speaking without inflection, 'will tell you that the last sacraments are a notorious pick-me-up. Well, I've had them and so you may believe that I am in full possession of my faculties when I tell you . . .'

What she proceeded to tell made disturbing sense.

Back in the anteroom, Anne, dazed and eager to doubt the old woman's words, sat trying to steady herself with coffee. She felt feverish and light-headed as if in the incubating stages of flu. Bruni had left a bottle of grappa next to the coffee pot and she poured some into her cup, making a *caffè corretto*, then wished she hadn't as it reminded her of the Arezzo bar and Franco. She felt as if her stores of judgement had been dissipated and used up.

Across the room, the monsignor was listening to Neri with half an ear and shooting glances at her. He, Niccolosa had promised, had a sealed letter to give her which would dissolve all her doubts.

'Does *he* know?' Anne had asked, feeling sceptical of Niccolosa. 'Does anyone but you?'

'He guesses,' the old woman told her. 'He puts two and two together, but what he puts together he learned under the seal of the confessional, so he can neither tell what he knows nor be sure what it means.' A faint embryo of a smile sketched itself on Niccolosa's mouth. 'He's a good man,' she said, 'but a gossip. Painfully inquisitive. This will drive him mad.'

At this, Anne had produced a quick, nervous spurt of laughter and felt the old woman's hand move in hers.

'You're very like me,' said Niccolosa. 'I saw that the day you came. I recognized myself – my young self – in you when you came into that dark room full of the old relatives who will soon be back. The funeral chorus I call them. Crows. Rooks. They'll be back to divide up what I leave them and to chatter over me. Oh, they'll be indignant with me for leaving you the villa. I don't want *that* divided, Anne. I want you to live on it and farm it. Will you?'

Anne, faced with telling a lie to the dying woman, tried to prevaricate but Niccolosa was not deceived.

'You're shilly-shallying,' she accused. 'You have a mental reservation. Some secret. I know. I know you, you see. You are me!'

Her eyes were sharp, fierce, focused and very recessed in the grey hollows of her waxen face. Anne wondered whether this was the last bright flame before the old woman flickered out. She was terrified at the thought. She couldn't bear to be the last one to speak to Niccolosa. Indeed, at this moment, she could hardly speak at all. Her tongue, momentarily, seemed to have turned to wood.

'That may depend on Guido,' she managed to say.

'Guido, yes. Where is he? Why isn't he here?'

'He's coming. He phoned from Zurich to say he's on his way.'

'Well,' said his mother, 'he'd better hurry.'

Some time later Ida walked into the anteroom where Anne was pondering all this.

'The Marchese Guido is on the phone,' she said. 'He's at the airport in Pisa and wants to talk to the Signorina.'

'Say you can't find me,' Anne pleaded. She couldn't face him now. The numbing paralysis which had started in her tongue had begun creeping coldly down her limbs. Her mouth felt as if she had been to the dentist and she could hardly get out these few words to Ida. 'Let him give you any message he needs to,' she begged. 'Please, Ida. Say I went for a walk.'

They were all looking at her: Ida, Bruni, Neri and the monsignor. This, said their surprised looks, was indiscreet and wilful: scandalous behaviour at such a time. She would have to talk to him.

She couldn't.

Ida waited.

Anne burst into tears.

'Well, all right,' said Ida and left. *'Va be', va be'.'*

The others gathered round Anne, agreeing that she was too sensitive and ought, perhaps, to go to bed. The monsignor gave her a shrewd stare. Now that she was crying it was impossible to stop. She cried for Niccolosa, Franco and herself, then, blinded by the lights which fractured in the lens of her tears, groped her way down the corridor to her own room where she lay, still crying, in a very hot bath, trying to dissolve a knot which seemed to swell and harden inside her, so that she felt as if she had swallowed or grown pregnant with a stone.

'You're Guido's daughter,' Niccolosa had said and stared as if Anne were a freshly made acquisition on the Monopoly board. She had stared at her this way before, but now it made sense. *'That*'s why we're alike. You're a throw-back to me,' said the old lady who was the living and dying proof that sins of pride and vanity outlive all others. The lines on her face looked as though they had been picked out with a lead pencil. 'You're judicious, practical and controlled. Not at all like Guido, Neri or indeed your mother. No. You're me, Anne, myself as I used to be. I'm not mad. I have the proof. Or rather the monsignor has. It's a letter sent to me by your mother shortly before she died, though she must have prepared it long before. It's all there. Dates. Your blood group. Proof that your legal father was not in Ireland when you were conceived. I gather that *he* never knew or preferred not to. He was told you were a seven-month child but the records show that you weighed seven pounds, so this is unlikely. She amassed it all carefully and now the monsignor has it. Sealed. I had planned to tell Guido first, but when he came to the hospital he was argumentative about the legacy. He wore me out and the doctor made him leave before I could get round to this. Now he's not here and may not be back in time for me to tell him, so I'm telling *you.* You must tell him for me, Anne, if I don't get a chance to myself. Show him the mark on your left shoulder. I saw it one day when you wore a sun dress and he'll know it too. It's a distinctively shaped freckle which all our family have somewhere on their bodies. You see, your feeling for him – and his for you – was not what you thought. It can't and must not be.' The glare of Niccolosa's intent eyes cut at Anne like slits of dark metal. 'Do you understand?'

'No,' begged Anne hopelessly. Hope was withering as, through wavering incredulity, she recognized the stubborn stringency of Fate. 'I *can't* believe any of this.'

'It will sink in.' Niccolosa closed her clam-grey eyelids. Snap. 'It took me a while to accept it too,' she went on without opening them. 'I had the letter from your mother for a month before I could bring myself to write to you. Read it. You'll be convinced. If the family contests my will, you may have to use it. I'd rather you didn't. Scandal. These things are best kept within the family. That's why I didn't even tell the monsignor. Kiss me,' she ordered. 'I'm getting weaker and I have to speak to the others. Send Ida back in please when you leave.'

Anne's kiss aroused no response in the sunken flesh of Niccolosa's face. Like a creature hibernating, the dying woman was using up as little of her energy as she could manage – or perhaps reach.

Anne took a long, careful look at the closed eyes and face, then left the room and gave Ida her patient's message.

She was still lying in her cooling bath when, through the window, she heard a car crunch on the gravel below. Then a second one. Guido? Maria-Cristina? Grabbing a bath towel, she climbed on to a stool in an effort to see out of the bathroom window. But it was too small and too high. Dressing quickly, she threw cold water on her puffed face and went back to the anteroom.

Here nothing seemed to have changed. The monsignor and

Neri were still talking in one corner. Ida was resting on a couch and Bruni had just cleared away the bowls and cups and was wheeling the trolley from the room.

'The marchese and marchesa,' he told Anne, 'are with her now.'

As he spoke, the doctor came out of the sickroom. 'You may be needed soon,' he told the monsignor. They want to be alone with her for a minute first. They're hoping for a last word, but I'm afraid they're too late.'

He went into the corridor.

Neri stood up. 'I'm going in there,' he said. 'After all, she is my grandmother.'

The monsignor watched the door close after him. He turned to Anne. 'Kin,' he said.

'Yes.'

'This is for you.' He drew an envelope from his bag and handed it over. 'She never said what was in it.'

Anne took it silently.

'There will be talk about the legacy to you,' he said. 'It may be unpleasant.'

'You think I should refuse?'

'Oh,' he recoiled. 'I didn't say that. It's just that you should be prepared for trouble. She may be a little ... unsettled just now. A touch ...'

'*Non compos mentis?*'

'Well it's true she seemed very lucid but, well, if there were a *reason*, some explanation ... then people would understand.'

'Unless it were something they couldn't be told.'

'Ah.' His eye quickened. It was a soft, blackberry eye but bright as a bird's. 'Knowledge which nobody has is ineffective. You might say it doesn't exist.'

Contrary and out of control, a demon voice took over Anne's tongue.

'But what if I married Guido,' asked the demon voice insolently. 'Wouldn't that make the legacy all right? Legitimate?' The word tripped her. Guido, in there, flanked by two witnesses, must be discovering about illegitimacies and obstacles right now – unless his mother was past speaking? Wasn't that what the doctor had implied? Anne could then keep mum for ever. Marry him. Could she? Why not? What did people have against incest anyway? One like this which was surely purified by time and ignorance? The word's bad associations had to do with child-molesting and could not apply here. Niccolosa, practical as she prided herself on being, would surely have seen this if she had been truly in her right mind! So why not, then, why *not*?

The monsignor, suspecting all this, was about to tell her.

His hands, rising as if he were saying mass, flew apart in a benedictory gesture – unless it was one of horror? Or perplexity? His face was tight. *Not* benedictory then. '*If* there were a prior relationship,' he murmured, 'which could explain the legacy, that might preclude marriage, mightn't it?' He was scrutinizing her. 'Not *legally*,' he went on, 'but there would be your conscience. Then – always *if* this were so, there would be the danger with offspring, issue ...'

'There need be no issue.' The word confused her. She forgot which sense she had meant it to have. 'We are being too allusive, you and I,' she told him. 'We're lost in a forest of "ifs".' It struck her that *if* was the French for yew tree, and the odd, involuntary pun took her up short. An omen? Of what? Yews were cemetery trees. Of death then? But surely there was no need for omens announcing *that*? 'I've learned,' she told him, 'that the two vital rules in a family like this one are to keep patrimonies intact and preserve appearances. A marriage between Guido and me would do both.' The demon inside her had definitely got the upper hand. But what I said is true, she thought, then remembered that Guido might be learning of the impediment even now. He would never defy it. How could he with Maria-Cristina and Neri knowing of it as well? She strained to hear whether anything was being said in the sickroom, but couldn't catch a sound.

'Neri,' said the monsignor, changing the subject, 'is thinking of going abroad for a year to do social work. A lot of young people do that nowadays.'

'Yes.' Still no sound.

'You look like her,' said the monsignor, suddenly, and stared intently at Anne. 'It's in the expression of the mouth. The eyes ... something striking.'

Then he was looking past her. He stood up and Anne, turning round, saw that Guido had appeared at the sickroom door. He beckoned the monsignor who walked in past him. Guido gave Anne a tired nod. 'She's gone,' he said. 'She was as good as dead when I got here. She never knew me and never said a word.'

The day of the funeral was so sunny that silhouettes split in two, roads liquified in a mirage of molten heat and the white Carrara marble in the graveyard shone like tin. Anne pondered her plans. The dead woman and she had complex accounts to settle, but decision rests with the living.

A rumour must have got out about the legacy for the mourners kept darting curious glances at her. The will was to be read that afternoon.

Anne kept talking to the dead woman in her mind. 'I would only be putting your own precepts into practice,' she argued with her. 'You were frightened of a word. A mirage. "Incest". Yet you wanted to set right the past – well, what better way? Surely, you can see that? What good is a father to me now? I'm twenty-two. What I want is a husband.'

A buffet lunch had been laid out in the villa and when the mourning figures gathered round it, Anne was reminded of

Niccolosa's comparing them to crows. They seemed more like starlings to her: twittery, chattery, moving about in sudden darts and plunges.

When Neri brought her a plate of food, she asked, 'Am I at all like your grandmother?'

Neri didn't think the question odd. This was Niccolosa's day.

'Like her when she was young, you must mean? Maybe. You've lost that Northern greyness.'

'Greyness! Thanks a lot!'

'I liked it,' he told her. 'To us the North is romantic: women in heavy wool, stiff upper lips, toast. Everything crisp and closed to repel that misty seepage that erodes boundaries and makes ghosts and souls merge into each other as pigments do in Impressionist paintings. Marvellous murk.'

'That was soot.'

'Soot?'

'Pollution. *Inquinamento*. A thing of the past. Air used to be black. The fusc and dimness came from a technological lack: no electricity.'

'You *are* like my grandmother,' said Neri. 'Literal-minded.'

'Or crisply Nordic?'

'Too crisp. I've gone off all that, anyway. I'm off to the steamy tropics. For a year. Will you be my stepmother when I come back?'

'Maybe.'

'Well, I'll be happy to miss the wedding.' Neri moved off to talk to an aunt.

Another mourner, a stray whom Anne had observed nibbling on the edge of different groups, came and attached herself. Anne, she was sure, wouldn't remember her, but they had met here at the little memorial for Flavia. Less than a month ago! Who would have expected another sad occasion so soon? Her name was the Contessa Bini and, while Anne was remembering that Niccolosa had herself expected it, she began to talk of Maria-Cristina.

'Radiant, isn't she? Black suits her – and she's waited a long time for this day. Niccolosa wouldn't hear of a divorce between her and Guido.'

'Does she want one?'

'My dear, you don't think she's been alone while he was gallivanting about? Of course, she's had to be discreet. But that's easier than you might think. We have a saying: "She who at first a good name gets, may piss abed and say she sweats." Haha! A little indelicate, but life *is*, don't you think? Also secretive! Who was the Frenchman who said that language was given to mankind so as to conceal thought? I've always thought *that* very wise.'

After a while the gossipy contessa moved off and Anne, left alone, turned the barbed words over in her mind and wondered whether the barbs were meant to hurt her or were for her use. The woman could possibly have brought a message from Maria-Cristina.

The wine being served was the same cool, white Arbia that she and Guido had drunk in Fiesole. She had a glass and then another one and when at last she saw Guido heading towards her – he had been busy until now with his duties as chief mourner – the air around him was so tremulous with wickery tricks of light that he looked like a figure crowned with a wreath. They smiled at each other and she decided to follow the old saws.